IT MIGHT HAVE BEEN WHAT HE SAID

IT MIGHT HAVE BEEN WHAT HE SAID

A NOVEL

EDEN COLLINSWORTH

ARCADE PUBLISHING
NEW YORK

FIRST EDITION

Excerpt from *Collected Poems 1909–1962* by T. S. Eliot, © 1936 by Harcourt, Inc., and renewed 1964 by T. S. Eliot, reprinted by permission of the publisher

This is a work of fiction. Names, places, characters, and incidents are either products of the author's imagination or are used fictitiously.

Library of Congress Cataloging-in-Publication Data
Collinsworth, Eden.
 It might have been what he said : a novel / by Eden Collinsworth. —1st ed.
 p. cm.
ISBN 1-55970-812-3
1. Publishers and publishing—Fiction. 2. Psychological fiction. I. Title.
PS3603.O4564I86 2006
813'.6—dc22   2005029598

Published in the United States by Arcade Publishing, Inc., New York
Distributed by Time Warner Book Group

Visit our Web site at www.arcadepub.com

10   9   8   7   6   5   4   3   2   1

EB

PRINTED IN THE UNITED STATES OF AMERICA

For Gilliam
and
To Bob Hodes

Reason, your viceroy in me, me should defend,
But is captiv'd . . .

—John Donne

IT MIGHT HAVE BEEN WHAT HE SAID

1

Isabel couldn't remember why she tried to kill
her husband . . .
it might have been what he said.

1

Isabel could remember the precise moment she tried killing her husband. Strangely enough, she couldn't recall why.

"How do you think of yourself?" asked the psychiatrist.

Without hesitating Isabel answered, "In three parts."

"And they are . . . ?"

"Mind; heart; sex," said Isabel.

"Is that the order of their importance?"

"Not necessarily . . ."

"So there isn't one that's more important than the other two?"

Isabel was becoming irritated by the psychiatrist and his line of questioning.

"No," she replied. "But I sometimes consider my heart and sex to be instigators. When that happens, I depend on my intelligence to keep everything in perspective."

"It seems to me that you've suggested your mind is the most important part of you," proposed the psychiatrist.

"I wasn't 'suggesting' anything." Isabel's impatience was edging its way toward contempt. "What I said was clear. Intelligence saves me by stepping in, sometimes at the last moment, with the 'yes, but . . .'"

"Evidently not this time," said the doctor.

Isabel's haughtiness was the thin ice covering bottomless self-doubt.

She appeared in control . . . she was anything but. She didn't want to talk about the desperate state she was in; circumstances left her no choice. Isabel distrusted psychiatrists. She stared unflinchingly at this one and — despite his years of professional training — made him feel uncomfortable. The doctor hoped it appeared otherwise. He continued the interview. "Why? Why murder when there were other choices?"

"I don't remember," was her answer.

It was the simple and complicated truth.

Isabel's failure to recall what prompted her to attempt murder was ironic — it was supremely ironic because, in addition to a rational disposition, Isabel had a photographic memory. Like a camera, her eye captured images of what she had seen; like a photo album, her mind enabled her to recollect her past in exact detail.

"Where was your ability to reason, then, Isabel, when you lost yourself in such an irrational act?" asked the psychiatrist.

"I don't know," said Isabel.

"All right . . . let's concentrate on now. Where's your memory now, when it's crucial to recall the circumstances?"

"I don't know," she repeated.

Isabel was just as confounded by her dire situation as the psychiatrist. Neither understood they were chasing false leads. Isabel's motive for murder wouldn't be pieced together in images. It would be found at the end of a trail of words.

The psychiatrist wasn't entirely wrong. Isabel did in fact place trust in the one part of herself that was her analytic intelligence. She had always imagined it living in a separate place, away from overreaching sentiments and appetites.

"Describe how it works," said the doctor.

"What?"

"Your memory. Explain, step by step, how you retain everything you read or see. Let's use the example of a document. If I ask you about a certain clause in a document, what happens?"

"The images appear in sequence," explained Isabel, "from general to specific. First comes the designated page; and then the paragraph; then the specific clause."

Isabel's mental route was circuitous but effective: as long as she processed memory by what she had seen, she could remember anything. What Isabel omitted telling the psychiatrist was far more revealing: she dreamed with the same visual clarity.

The night before her wedding, Isabel had a dream that lasted the brief time it took to convey a simple scene: her future husband, in the back seat of a limousine, driven away as she was left standing on the curb of an unknown street. It was a short dream, taking only a few conscious seconds, but its details refracted like distinctly colored shards of glass. What was odd was its vantage point, as though whatever happened was being witnessed from above. She woke with such foreboding, she was sure the dream would become real. Eventually it did.

Fifteen years later, just as it was in the dream, her husband left her standing on the curb of a street as he was driven away. Isabel was unable to see through the limousine's tinted windows and wondered whether he was looking straight at her, or if he had fixed his eyes ahead. The car pulled away, exactly as it had in the dream. The street on which she was left, unrecognizable at the time of the premonition, was the street in front of their New York apartment where — two floors above — their son was watching from the window.

It was starkly final. Her husband had left her. Isabel denied it, but their twelve-year-old son knew. He saw it from the window in his room. Isabel witnessed exactly what her son had, but her entire being rejected the fact of it. Weeks passed. There was no alternative but to accept reality. By then, Isabel no longer consisted of three equal parts. Immeasurable despair had reduced her to only one — a disabled heart.

Not satisfied with consuming her by grief from within, her unmoored heart became dead matter pressing down on her chest from the outside. Whatever was left of Isabel was struggling to escape from beneath its crushing weight.

Forced to choose between what she felt and what she knew, Isabel decided her ability to reason was her sole source of rescue. In the only way she understood to find her bearings, Isabel reconstructed their relationship in sequence, from background to foreground: She met James. She loved James. She married James. They had a child together. They made a life together. What had happened next? What went so abruptly wrong that she would try to kill him? Not infidelity. They were then, as they had always been, the most intimate lovers. She loved him unquestionably at the time she tried killing him. It wasn't her formidable mind that drove her to it — she was known for her intelligent calm. No one part of her seemed responsible.

Isabel was sure that if she could accurately remember what happened in that murderous moment, it would explain what preceded and followed. Much like the page in which the contractual clause had been embedded, her mind's eye required a visual landscape that would trigger the process of remembering. But something was wrong. Her brain — utterly dependable until now — offered Isabel nothing. There was no delineated shape of what had happened . . . only a blur. There was no vivid color to her memory . . . only white rage. Isabel had seen what she had seen at the time it happened — she was sure of that. Pictures had been snapped, but for some unknown reason her brain refused to develop them.

After great effort, Isabel brought forth one clear image. It was James's expression of stunned confusion the moment he felt her first blow. She started with his expression of disbelief and worked backward to remember the rest.

2

Isabel Simpson had always known who she was . . . and that who she was had been due, in large part, to her upbringing.

As children, Isabel and her brother, Ian, rarely saw their parents, separately or together. Semi-strangers supervised their entire childhood.

These facts had laid the foundation for a gothic plot waiting to be parodied. But there were two narrative devices in particular Isabel, the editor, would have flagged as literary clichés worthy enough to be considered camp. One was her childhood home: a lugubrious mansion overlooking Lake Michigan. It had been built at the turn of the century with a fortune made in meatpacking, and bought by Isabel's father with his own fortune from the steel industry. The other was Vera: a forbiddingly Teutonic nanny assigned to Isabel and her brother.

Uniformed from head to toe in stiff whites, Vera was violently impatient with life's small frustrations. She loathed children, whom she identified as untidy and disruptive. That the Simpsons were able to ignore Vera's disturbing personality traits in hiring her underscored their profound remove from parenthood.

The limited discourse Vera had with her charges hinged on one coarse command, "Es ist verboten." Acting instinctively on her peasant wits, Vera knew the boy could be easily handled: he was trusting of adults. But the silent girl who stared at her without blinking was an entirely different matter. Vera recognized Isabel as trouble.

Given the opportunity, Dr. Lewis would no doubt pontificate that most children have a defining experience — one that shapes and predetermines a perception of their world. Isabel's moment occurred while she was waiting to have her mouth washed out by Vera. Why her mouth was washed out with soap would never be clear to Isabel — that day or any other. But she would always be able to remember the quick yank of her arm and flash of steps as she was dragged down to the basement. The faint smell of linseed oil that had recently polished a wooden step stool needed to reach the laundry sink. The soft texture of a bath towel worn like an enormous bib to protect her hand-embroidered smock dress from the messiness of what was to come.

If ever there was a test of Isabel's resolve, it happened standing on that stool in the semi-dark, waiting for Vera to return from the gardener's pantry with a bar of pumice soap. Sentenced to punishment for an unexplained infraction, Isabel gazed down to the bottom of the sink and realized she was at the mercy of adults who, despite their respectable appearances, were arbitrarily dangerous.

Ian, two years older than Isabel, was a nervous child who slept under his bed rather than in it. Nighttime was a drain trap for his daytime anxieties, and the floor seemed more solid ground than the mattress. One less bed to make was reason enough for the maid to keep the boy's abnormal sleeping habits to herself.

It happened that Ian was having problems of his own the day Isabel had her mouth washed out. The cook had casually mentioned that he and his sister were joining their parents for dinner.

Panicked by the unexpected news, Ian looked everywhere in the large house for Isabel before expanding his search to the gardens.

"Isabel . . . where *are* you?" he called out, doing his best to hold back tears.

Isabel was perched on a black iron bench, sipping lemonade to rid the residual soap taste from her mouth. Distance prevented her from hearing all his words, but the pitched timbre of Ian's voice announced his upset.

"I'm here, Ian," Isabel called back before sighting him. Having just come around the tall hedges, he was now running down the garden's long vista toward her.

Arriving out of breath, scratched by a shortcut through the rosebushes, determined not to let his younger sister see him cry, Ian stood in front of Isabel and balefully repeated one question —

"Where will I put my hand?"

It sounded like a personalized version of the riddle of the Sphinx, but Ian's question was rooted in a real issue that caused him untold grief. Of all the people in Ian's life, only Isabel understood his dilemma. He had been born left-handed. . . .

Worse yet, Ian was forced to become right-handed. The decision to convert had to do with Vera's misguided perspective, which, unfortunately for Ian, hadn't progressed beyond medieval superstition that the left hand was an instrument of the devil.

Vera was brutishly determined to correct what she was sure was an onerous situation. Ian's confused and lank right hand was required to open and close scissors for hours at a time, so that its strength might improve. It filled practice notebooks with hopelessly illegible handwriting. Everything was done to shore up the use of his right hand and simultaneously discourage his left each time it instinctively tried to assist. After months of retraining, Ian managed to will his brain and hands to work in artificial tandem.

But just barely. Like a disgraced army general, his strong left hand was forced to abdicate command to the subordinate right hand. And his right hand, like a fatigued infantryman, was pushed into battle after exhausting battle without any ability to lead.

The dreaded news of dinner that night presented yet another level of hand doubt for Ian. Vera insisted Ian's left hand was to hold his plate; but when eating with his parents, he had been castigated for not keeping it face up on his napkined lap. To make matters even more complicated, his mother had recently changed the rules by instructing the children to eat in the European manner, wherein both hands work simultaneously.

"Izzie, Vera has never been invited to eat with Mother and Father at the dining room table," Ian correctly pointed out at one time. "I'm sure it's because she hasn't gotten her hands right yet," he reasoned.

Unlike her brother, Isabel understood why her parents would never invite Vera to dine with them. It was because Vera's place was not at their table. But there was a corresponding factor to be weighed: Isabel recognized long ago that her mother had subcontracted the children to the staff. It would be naive to think of Vera in a marginalized position, regardless of where she ate her meals.

"What if there was no one method?" suggested Isabel. What if they simply adjusted to the variables imposed by each of the three different grown-ups making the rules?

"What do you mean?" blurted Ian with a look divided equally between consternation and fear.

"Let's try something," said Isabel. "Tonight we eat with Mother and Father, so tonight we'll put our hands in our laps." She reassured her brother, "Just watch me when you get confused."

Ian listened intently to Isabel and tried to follow what she was saying.

"Tomorrow morning, when we have breakfast with Vera, hold your plate with the hand that's in your lap tonight," instructed Isabel. "Before we go to bed, I'll put a dot on the back of your lap hand. All you'll need to do if you forget which hand is which is to look for the dot."

Ian carefully considered his sister's proposal. It didn't involve outright defiance, which was good because defiance was simply not in his nature. But it seemed slightly disingenuous; the idea of cribbing from a pen mark on his hand reminded him of cheating. Ian couldn't absorb the moral consequences right then, but decided to agree to Isabel's scheme on blind faith. He wanted a way out, and Isabel seemed to have a map. If he couldn't follow it, he would follow her.

Ian was put to the test that night and at breakfast the following morning. Isabel's strategy spared him punishment both times. It was then that Ian placed his trust entirely in his sister's ability to navigate the swirling eddies of their childhood; and Isabel made a conscious decision to subjugate her emotions to the far more serious matter of prevailing.

3

Isabel's father, Rufus Simpson, was like a weather condition with its own physical properties.

Single-minded and ambitious, Mr. Simpson never had the slightest doubt about his place in the scheme of things. The nature and degree of his success instilled respect in men and adoration among women.

Mr. Simpson's corporation produced steel. His business travel resulted in long absences from the family. But even when he was at home, Rufus communicated with his two children by routing articles from the *New York Times* or the *Wall Street Journal*. Each clipping was attached to a cover note typed by Miss Drake, his secretary of many years:

```
         Dear Ian (or Isabel):
 I thought this would be of interest...
                  Father
              Enclosure(s)
```

Most of the world's steel came from integrated mills utilizing massive blast furnaces until Rufus recognized an opportunity in producing molten steel cost-effectively. He designed and built small-cylindered electric arc furnaces. They became known as mini-mills.

That allowed Rufus to manufacture concrete-reinforcing bars that became known as rebars. That provided Rufus a yet-to-be-tapped tier of the steel market . . . which generated a profit margin of 7 percent for a new product category . . . which ate into 4 percent of the industry's tonnage.

Rufus Simpson believed life was a race to be won, and he took personally anything impeding his progress. It did not prevent Mr. Simpson from being a courtly man. As a small child, Isabel noticed he would remove his hat in the elevator even if she were the only other passenger. At the same early age, Isabel knew her father to be as hard and cold as the steel that had built his fortune.

When — during a contentious labor strike — an anonymously menacing phone call was made to the Simpson home, Rufus invited the union leader for lunch at the Chicago Club. There was no mention of the unfortunate incident during the course of their meal. Afterward, Rufus led his guest from the club's dining room to its hushed library. Gesturing him to one of the French windows overlooking Wabash Avenue, Rufus asked nonchalantly, "Do you see that man — there — on the corner?"

"Yes," answered the unsuspecting union leader.

"He's been paid to permanently cripple you if any member of your union suggests the slightest discomfort to any member of my family. Am I understood?" was Rufus's second and only other question before excusing himself. "I think I'll leave you to a quiet moment. Just let my driver know where you'd like to be taken once you've collected yourself."

If Isabel's parents were cast as fictional characters, they'd appear in different novels: Mr. Simpson in one written by Theodore Dreiser; Mrs. Simpson in one by Zola. Shimmering in the distance like a beautiful mirage, Isabel's mother — Tisza — was as ethereal as Rufus Simpson was earthbound. Of undisclosed European background, Tisza Simpson had a maiden name and accent diffi-cult to place. In fact, everything about her was strangely elusive.

Mrs. Simpson took an extended holiday both times she gave birth, leaving alone and directly from the maternity ward. At home, she was her least comfortable in the company of her chil-dren; and in the unlikely event they ever saw her, very little was said. Ian and Isabel knew from television and their friends that a maternal relationship typically included contact with one's chil-dren, and that Mrs. Simpson presented a fairly unusual rendition of motherhood.

4

Dr. Lewis was a distinguished psychiatrist with a taxing lecture schedule and a private practice in New York. He spent Sunday afternoons at his office preparing for the coming week's appointments.

Only after he hung up the phone did it occur to him that the woman, Isabel Simpson, must have somehow known his routine.

"How can I help you?" the doctor asked Isabel after she introduced herself in person and was seated across from him.

Isabel responded with a question of her own.

"Is it true that in the middle of the brain there's something called the caudate?" she asked.

Adding to Dr. Lewis's intrigue was now bewilderment.

"The caudate nucleus." He pronounced the words with deliberate authority. "It occupies a relatively small section."

"Regardless of its size, it has a profound impact on behavior," said Isabel.

"You seem to be well versed on the subject."

"I've read that its cells produce a chemical that is released into the bloodstream when a person feels desire."

"Dopamine is the chemical, but whatever studies there've been have generally associated it with passion —"

"Passion and desire are inextricably linked," Isabel fired back.

Dr. Lewis wasn't used to being interrupted by a patient . . . especially when it concerned his area of clinical expertise.

"For the sake of your point, I'll agree. Exactly what is your point?" he asked.

"Don't you see? It's a kind of biochemical self-fulfilling prophecy," said Isabel. "The more desire one feels — and the more the object of desire is withheld — the more extreme one's behavior becomes."

"That's an unorthodox way of putting it; but, yes, I suppose the gist of what you've said is correct," said Dr. Lewis. "I'm still not getting your point."

Isabel's eyes locked on to Dr. Lewis. Her point gathered its full force. "Under certain circumstances, love looks like mental illness," she said.

Dr. Lewis thought the woman who phoned on a Sunday without a referral, much less an appointment — who faced him down with a defiant stare and ramrod posture — was capable of acting on any number of impulses . . . second-degree murder included.

Isabel's blunt candor had pile-driven down to bedrock: she admitted trying to kill her husband, but insisted she couldn't remember how or why. Before their second session, Dr. Lewis decided that, rather than focus on Isabel's murderous act, he would ask her to describe her relationship with her mother.

Isabel bristled when the question was asked.

"I had none," she said.

"How can that be?" asked Dr. Lewis.

"It can," said Isabel. "It was."

"Surely there were times when your mother sought you out?" suggested Dr. Lewis.

"Once, when I was a girl," said Isabel.

"What were the circumstances?" asked the doctor.

"I was practicing how to get in a car," answered Isabel.

"I didn't catch that," said Dr. Lewis.

"I was practicing —," repeated Isabel.

"To get in a car?" asked the doctor.

"Yes."

"Why would you need to practice?"

"To do it correctly," said Isabel.

"How wrong can one possibly be when it comes to getting in a car?"

"I've provided enough of my backstory for a better question than that," said Isabel sarcastically.

"Really?"

"It's the flip side . . . not how wrong, but how correct. How precisely correct can you be getting in a car? Manners are measured in degrees of subtle correctness," said Isabel. "Just as table manners were to be mastered, so too the manner I was to get in a car."

"I can't imagine. . . . Tell me," said Dr. Lewis.

It involved sitting down on the very edge of the car seat — facing out — feet planted on the pavement. Pushing off the pavement, Isabel was expected to propel herself to the middle of the seat and simultaneously pivot so as to end up facing forward. That Saturday afternoon, the car had been parked in the driveway in order for her to practice. No matter how many times the exercise was repeated, Isabel was unable to organize her disparate and gangly limbs to act in a single, seamless motion.

"You do realize how aggressively odd it was," said Dr. Lewis.

"What?" asked Isabel.

"The zeal by which propriety was enforced. The table manners . . . the car thing."

"Yes, I knew it was odd . . . but there was no choice."

"Fair enough," said Dr. Lewis. "What about that day."

"She was coming out of the house while I was getting in and out of the car," recounted Isabel. "It must have been a whim . . . she decided to take me along to the beauty parlor."

"And . . . ?" asked Dr. Lewis.

"I was thrilled."

"What did you talk about during the drive?"

"Nothing."

"Nothing?"

"That's right . . . nothing. But something happened when we arrived in front of the beauty parlor."

There was a long pause.

"Well, are you going to tell me?"

"Mother double-parked to wait for a car that was just pulling out . . . another driver came out of nowhere and usurped the parking space."

"And . . . ?"

"And that's when it happened."

Dr. Lewis leaned forward in his chair, then — realizing he was anticipating Isabel's response — sat back.

"She turned off the motor and adjusted her strand of pearls so its clasp was in the back," continued Isabel. "She said she'd just be a moment."

"'I'll just be a moment,' was all she said," Isabel repeated to herself.

Dr. Lewis leaned forward again, this time making no effort to mitigate the suspense.

Initially the exchange between her mother and the man appeared civil, explained Isabel. But he became progressively agitated the longer Mrs. Simpson calmly held her ground. The man stepped out of the car, and Isabel heard the word "bitch." She saw her mother slap the man across his face.

"Without any urgency whatsoever, mother walked to our car and slipped behind its wheel in one perfectly coordinated movement. She shut the door and sealed in such calm that, at first, I thought what I'd just witnessed hadn't really happened. But I looked out the window, and as we passed the man — standing in the exact location he'd been confronted — I saw what vouched for it. A bleeding skid mark across his face . . . Mother was wearing a loose ring that had turned itself around . . . the stone was facing in, and it tore his cheek."

"Did you and your mother discuss what happened?"

"No."

"Not during the drive to the house?"

"No," said Isabel to the psychiatrist. That's all you get today, she thought to herself.

Dr. Lewis realized there would be no more to Isabel's answer. As he wrote in his notepad, Isabel remembered that, despite her age at the time, she hadn't been squeamish about the man's gouged face. During the drive back to the house, she had busied her brain by compiling a mental inventory of books with the word *red* in their titles: *The Red Balloon, The Red Badge of Courage;* and what of *The Scarlet Letter* . . . not red exactly, but in the range. When she couldn't think of any more color-coded book titles, Isabel contemplated the slap. It was an act taken by a woman, occurring without regret, causing a man physical injury and public humiliation. Isabel had always considered her mother an impenetrable mystery . . . but the slap was proof of something her mother possessed that other mothers didn't seem to: the unqualified confidence in her station as a woman.

"I've had enough today," said Isabel.

"That's fine . . . our time was almost up," said Dr. Lewis whose scrawled notation concluded, *"repressed childhood . . . violent tendencies (same) from mother."*

5

When the gods grant gifts to a mortal, punishment isn't too far behind.

Isabel's memory came with the emotional cost measured by its cruel accuracy. One unrelenting torment had to do with a sound.

Not long after the incident in front of the beauty parlor, Isabel heard an unworldly sound. It had beckoned from the house's first-floor guest room. The Chintz Room faced south. Its flowered upholstery and hand-blocked English wallpaper of peacocks were almost always bathed in sun. On this particular day, the room's curtains were inexplicably drawn. Isabel cracked the door open to investigate, sending a chevron of light into the mystery — but not enough for her to see anything that would explain the sound.

"Is anyone here?" Isabel inquired to the darkness as she tentatively stepped inside the room. There was no answer . . . only more of the pitiless sound.

Isabel's curiosity turned into fear. What would continue wailing when it was aware of someone in the same room? It wasn't the sad — but recognizable — sound of weeping. More like a high-pitched cry made by a desperate animal trying to escape a trap by chewing off its own leg. She reached behind to push the door wide open. When the hall light flooded in, Isabel was able to see that the unholy sound and her mother were one and the same.

The day Isabel discovered the unspeakable reason for the sound was the day she watched her mother being borne away. Isabel was almost the age her son would be when he saw his father, under different circumstances, also disappear. And like her son, some thirty-five years later, Isabel witnessed her world change from a window view two floors above.

Hospital attendants, choreographed by a nurse whose crisp white uniform was not dissimilar to that of Vera's, engineered her mother into the back seat of a car that looked like a fortress on wheels. Isabel opened a window on the house's second-floor hall overlooking the scene, so that she might hear what was being said. But the adults — who seemed to have been programmed in advance — were moving mutely in concert from one reverent task to the other. The only noise was of driveway gravel. First, the crunching of it underfoot. Then, the dissipating pelting of it against the wheels of the car, which faded from sight.

Isabel trained her eyes on the car until it was no longer within the frame of the window. After the last sight of her mother — the car as a speck at the end of the driveway was all that was left to view — Isabel stepped away. She went into the bathroom and tucked herself in the narrow space between the toilet and the bathtub. Sitting on the floor, surrounded by cool white porcelain, Isabel drew up her long legs and wrapped her arms around them. She put her head down on her knees, closed her eyes, and balanced her mind on only two words. If Isabel recited the words to herself, she was able to break loose from the devastating horror that had hidden itself in the Chintz Room. By repeating two words, Isabel reduced herself to all that mattered, and all that mattered could be launched into limitless space. One word said after the other, then repeated: *Let go* . . .

Soon after Mrs. Simpson was institutionalized, the children were separated from one another and sent to boarding schools in different foreign countries. They were told their mother had an inner ear infection and needed rest. Ian — having no understanding of the situation and afraid of pressing his father for details — accepted the absurdly false explanation. Isabel sheltered her brother by keeping the secret. But it was only one of many. Like the smallest in a grouping of intricately painted Russian dolls, that single secret had been crafted to nestle neatly within one, then another, and then another ornately concealed secret.

6

Background is a poor substitute for character but shouldn't be completely ignored because, inevitably, it explains a thing or two.

Rufus Simpson came from a seriously questionable background. His English forebears, two brothers who barely escaped execution in the early 1700s, were what would now be referred to as career criminals. The prisons were full; luck saved them with a choice between hanging and boarding a trading ship bound for America.

Both men settled in the Appalachian Mountains and became trappers. Simpson offspring gradually migrated to the East Tennessee Valley. Rufus's brash uncle, Sherman Simpson, made a fortune as a bootlegger. After a stint at Leavenworth for liquor smuggling, he opened a New York City speakeasy. When Prohibition was repealed, it became a famous nightclub and the favorite gathering spot for café society.

Sherman refused to cooperate with the mob's protection racket and was murdered. But it wasn't organized crime that killed Sherman. It was his reckless manhood. While he was chatting with Walter Winchell one night at the club's corner banquette, a recently cuckolded husband walked over to greet them . . . his welcoming handshake held tight to Sherman's, while the other, holding a gun, shot point-blank into his face.

Isabel's father was an only child — orphaned early — who lived with Uncle Sherman's spinster sister. Rufus escaped the oppression of his aunt and the South by way of a train ticket and Harvard, both paid for by Uncle Sherman. Like his uncle, Rufus was a maverick. He wasn't interested in membership in any one particular university house. Instead, he struck a distribution agreement with the Coca-Cola Company to install vending machines in all of Harvard's houses. By the time he graduated, Rufus had made the first of his many fortunes.

Despite their parents' absence, Isabel and her brother were tightly controlled. They were required to excel in two social sports — tennis and sailing — and were assigned a third, gender-specific activity. For Isabel, it was ballet. For Ian, it was boxing taught at the Chicago Athletic Club. Even in the locker room, the coach addressed Ian as "Mr. Simpson." The boy's courteous replies were prefaced with "Sir."

The children's lives were dictated by an immutable code of behavior that appeared admirable. But decorum took the place of something that should have been slightly more human.

"The world will call on you, Isabel," Mr. Simpson told his daughter just before she walked down the ramp and into a plane. Isabel was twelve years old at the time.

The plane would take her from Ian and to an isolated life at boarding school in Zurich.

Her father said it at the gate, instead of "Good-bye." He reached up to his brown Borsalino hat, removed it, and said, "The world will call on you, Isabel. I expect you to meet its challenges head-on.

"You must always remain a lady," he added with the same weight of importance.

Rufus Simpson put his hat back on, turned around, and walked away.

7

Long before Mrs. Simpson was sent to a mental hospital, long before Isabel and Ian left for boarding schools, they were told their mother was Lutheran and their father was southern.

"Something's wrong," Isabel suggested to Ian.

"Why?" asked Ian.

"Well, Mother's religion is described by a word that must mean whatever it is," Isabel laid out her argument, "but Father's religion is described by a general direction. Don't you think that's strange?"

"Maybe by being southern, you practice the only religion there," speculated Ian. "Maybe you don't have a choice."

"That can't be it," insisted Isabel. "Something's missing. They're not telling us something . . . some piece of information that's important."

Identifying her religion was fairly academic because, with the exception of Christmas and Easter, Isabel hadn't been inside a church. That was fine by her. She was not God-fearing by nature. Then, for reasons unexplained, Mrs. Simpson decided the children should attend the Episcopal Sunday school in town.

There was an incident during the children's first — and what would be their only — day of attendance. Rather than crayon in the outlined drawing of Jesus distributed by the teacher, Isabel insisted on a blank piece of paper so that she might render a personalized image of Christ. Ian became anxious. He knew his sister was capable of her own understated brand of disruption.

Confronting what appeared to be a polite child, the pastor was caught off guard by Isabel's refusal to follow the simple assignment.

"Why won't you color in the shapes?" he asked.

"Has anyone actually seen Jesus?" Isabel answered with a question.

"Yes, all those he has touched," he said.

"If we don't know what Jesus looks like, then he looks like whatever we imagine him to be. So why should I color in someone else's shape of him?"

Isabel was issuing a challenge more than posing a spiritual question. It was as though her entire nature, restless from being kept in check, chose to rebel against authority in a black outline of Christ.

"Whatever Jesus looks like doesn't matter. The only thing that matters, really, is if you believe in him or not," Isabel suggested to the other children, who had pegged her early in the lesson as an outside agitator. Isabel was sent home with a note memorializing her disrespect. Ian had been offered the opportunity to stay the course, but felt his sister deserved his loyalty. The Episcopal Sunday school didn't invite either of them back.

It was one more irony in Isabel's childhood that when her mother was institutionalized, in a manner of speaking, so too was Isabel. With his wife in a mental hospital in Chicago and an increasing amount of his business in Europe, Mr. Simpson established another base in London. Isabel was sent to a Catholic boarding school in Switzerland run by a very strict order of French nuns. During the years she attended, Isabel endured every conceivable version of being forced to color inside the shapes. At fifteen, she returned to America to enter Miss Porter's School for Girls. The imprimatur of a prestigious university for both children was the final benchmark established by their father.

Affected by anything and everything, Ian didn't adjust to life as well as his sister. For the better part of his childhood, he stood on constant guard, nervously waiting for the other metaphoric shoe to drop. At the same time Isabel was sent to the French nuns, Ian had been shipped off to the Dragon School, which was a "feeder" to Marlborough School. Both were unforgiving examples of the British public school tradition.

Rufus Simpson, that man of great wealth independently acquired, believed an individual shouldn't be dependent on advantages provided by birth. Isabel and Ian were told by their father that their college tuition marked his last parental obligation. Upon their graduation, the bank vault closed. Given the family resources, Isabel considered her father's dictum paradoxical. She assumed, as a daughter, she'd be allowed more leeway. No such sentimental dispensation was made. It was Mr. Simpson's belief that only economic self-sufficiency released women from subordination.

Ian moved to the most remote area of South America and became a cowboy. Mr. Simpson was appalled at what he considered the waste of a splendid — and expensive — education; but there was nothing to be done. Ian had chosen another direction, and it was far off the beaten path. He lived thousands of miles from his father's judgment, but the peace of mind denied in childhood continued to elude him as an adult. There was, however, something to be said about Ian's retreat to the middle of nowhere: he was finally able to offer his left hand its natural place at the table.

Words had saved Isabel's childhood from total unhappiness. Reading offered the fellowship lacking in her remote family. It was no surprise that words were the currency in which Isabel traded as an adult. She began her career as a receptionist in a book publishing company. Each night, after everyone else left the office, Isabel stayed to read the files.

8

Monina Immordino was a literary agent. She discovered young writers in the 1950s and '60s who, by the '90s, had become standard-bearers.

Monina made an indelible mark on the cultural landscape, but she never allowed herself to be influenced by money or fame; nor was she ever pulled off course by the power of her position. The fact that she was a recluse added to her legend.

Their introduction occurred after business hours. Isabel was in the office reading files when the telephone rang.

"Hello, this is Monina Immordino," she announced in such a deep voice Isabel thought the caller to be a man.

"How do you do, this is Isabel Simpson. I'm afraid everyone's left."

"Who are you again?"

"The receptionist."

"I didn't mean a title, I meant a name. Say your name again."

"Isabel Simpson."

"Can you find your way to the contract files, Isabel Simpson?"

"Yes, I know where to find the contract files."

"I'm phoning from the country, and my staff has left for the day. I want you to pull the most recent Gaddis contract and read me what's called an option clause. It should be the second to the last page. I'll wait."

As it happened, Isabel had recently read the "G" files.

"His contract dated June of 1974 grants the right of first refusal based on a twenty-page outline," Isabel said. "It also grants a ten percent topping privilege if we're unable to come to terms and you submit elsewhere."

Monina gave life to a dead silence. "Which is it . . . an exceptional memory or a delusional personality?"

"Given my gene pool —" Isabel stopped herself in mid-sentence. "Might I ask why you're calling for this information after business hours?"

Monina realized Isabel was on to her.

"That sounds like a rhetorical question," she said.

"Well, yes, I suppose it is. Is Mr. Gaddis dissatisfied?"

"Why ask that?"

"Because contracts only come into play when there's an unhappy party. You wouldn't be inquiring about his legal obligations if he intended to stay."

"You're right on both counts," said Monina.

"I guess your next question is if there's an arbitration clause," said Isabel.

The long pause that followed suggested to Isabel that she might have overstepped herself.

Finally Monina spoke.

"Is there?" she asked.

"None, as I recall," said Isabel. "Would you like me to double-check?"

"I doubt that's necessary. But tell me, why does a receptionist care whether Bill Gaddis comes or goes?"

"Because he's a brilliant writer, and this receptionist will not stay a receptionist," was Isabel's response.

"Well, then, we had better get to know each other. Come to my apartment next Wednesday at seven thirty. One-twenty East Seventeenth Street," instructed Monina.

Because none of her clients answered questions about her, and no one in the business would betray her privacy, there was never any press on Monina. She communicated with publishers only when absolutely necessary. Monina saw her writers, the small staff in New York, and a few locals in the Connecticut hamlet where she secluded herself most of the week. No one had been inside her apartment or house. Isabel's invitation to meet Monina was unusual. That it was taking place at Monina's apartment qualified as unprecedented.

The address turned out to be a brownstone. Isabel climbed the stairs and inspected names on its intercom. None were for Monina. Isabel walked back down the steps and opened the iron gate leading from the sidewalk to the ground-floor apartment. There was no buzzer to the door. She knocked . . . and waited for the great adventure that would answer.

Isabel had no idea what Monina looked like. Very few people did. But she certainly didn't expect the visual non sequitur that opened the door. The physical reality of Monina joyfully mocked any mental image one might have had of her. Standing in the doorway was a short, round woman in a gray, shapeless dress. Her hair was pulled back into a neat bun. She wore no makeup, and her only jewelry was a small gold cross around her neck. The ground-floor apartment suggested Monina to be more the Sicilian concierge than a renowned literary agent.

"You don't feed yourself enough," Monina said as they greeted each other.

Isabel walked into the apartment and onto floors completely covered by needlepoint rugs. There were countless rugs piled one on top of another. Not only were the rugs Monina's handiwork, so too were the pillows propped, like stacked tombstones, in every conceivable area where she would be likely to sit. Realizing Monina had cocooned her entire apartment in needlepoint, Isabel thought, Nowhere could possibly be stranger than where I am right now.

"Please sit. Would you like something to drink?" asked Monina politely.

"Just water, thank you."

Isabel sat down and pulled one of several pillows from behind her so she wasn't forced to balance on the edge of the couch. "My mother did the most remarkably intricate work in crewel," she said, looking at the pillow appreciatively.

"Your mother was European," Monina said while pouring herself a Canadian Club.

"How do you know that?"

"Unless you're misusing the word, crewel is a more refined stitch that is taught in Europe."

"She's still alive," volunteered Isabel.

Monina settled in a chair opposite Isabel. "And still insane?" she asked.

Monina had managed to get it right with nothing more than intuition. The word *insane* was harsh; but after guarding the secret for so many years, Isabel was relieved to have finally heard it spoken out loud. Then and there, she decided to trust Monina in a way she trusted no one else.

"They'd always take away her scissors." The sealed silence of the room, whose nearly floor-to-ceiling textiles buffered any outside noise, allowed Isabel's attention to drift. She smiled wistfully.

"You've remembered something," said Monina.

Isabel looked over at Monina, who had put down her drink.

"They took away . . . ," Isabel began to repeat. "No crewel in the hospitals. But they permitted large, clunky knitting needles," she continued. "When I was in boarding school, my mother mailed me a sweater knitted together in these gargantuan rows. She somehow doubled over the wool in order to accommodate her huge needles. The result was this unrecognizable garment that looked as if it had been on a regime of steroids. I was absolutely sure it was alive and growing during its trip by mail, because it was three times the size of the box it came in . . . and I swear it was undulating when I was finally able to pull it out. Mother didn't include a note. Or maybe she did, and the sweater ate it."

Monina's chuckling was infectious, and by the end of the story, Isabel was also laughing to the point of needing the bathroom.

"It's to the right, and the light is on the outside," said Monina.

Isabel stepped into the small bathroom. The shower curtain had been shredded into narrow strips. She decided it would be impolite to ask for an explanation. Unless Monina didn't bathe on a regular basis — highly improbable, given her appearance — Isabel concluded that whatever had happened was recent and had been done by someone else.

"You've seen what he left behind in the bathroom?" asked Monina, pouring herself another whisky before explaining. It seemed the only person to whom Monina had ever offered the apartment was one of her writers. His single oeuvre — a coming-of-age novel written in his early twenties — became prerequisite reading for American college students. What followed was an extended case of writer's block. He became furtively misanthropic and kept no home address. Every six months his royalty checks —

totaling hundreds of thousands of dollars — were sent to a P. O. box in Nova Scotia.

"I know he's going through a bad spell — well, it's been thirty years, so I suppose it's no longer a spell and now qualifies as his life — but if you take shears to someone else's shower curtain, decency dictates that you buy another," reasoned Monina as she prepared dinner: pasta with olive oil and pecorino cheese for Isabel; another whisky — this time mixed with milk — for herself. They spoke of many things; none had anything to do with book publishing. After Isabel cleaned her plate in the kitchen sink, she told Monina, "I should get home."

"I don't know what I'll do with Gaddis's next book," said Monina. "But I do know that someday you'll have a son, thin girl, and I'll love you both as my own."

Book publishing is a staid profession not given to meteoric ascents. Isabel was an exception. Her advancements — one after another — were due to a combination of attributes. Isabel possessed an ability to discover gifted writers, a genuine respect for their work, and a talent for editing what they wrote. Her determination demanded that all of these capabilities work together on behalf of unrelenting ambition. But it was pure luck that awarded Isabel her golden prize.

A stroke felled the company's president in the lobby of the University Club, and his head split open when it hit the marble floor. Isabel happened to be in the right place at the right time. At twenty-eight, she was given a chance to run the business. Lack of doubt provided a competitive advantage. Boundless energy fed her unapologetic drive. And a combination residing only in the young — ignorance and arrogance — eliminated any distraction along the way.

Isabel was prepossessing. That is certainly true. But no one who knew her thought Isabel to be self-satisfied, and so what came before her fall was more subtle than pride. Regardless of her early achievements, Isabel's life had taken place in the sanctuary of privilege, insulated by boarding schools and private country clubs. No amount of intelligence and intellectual self-reliance could make up for her lack of worldliness. That dangerous fact hid in the tall grass . . . and when it was eventually flushed out, Isabel didn't have the first idea of how to protect herself against its painful consequences.

9

Isabel's publishing company, Priam Books, was small but extremely profitable.

One of its best-selling mystery writers was the daughter of a past U.S. president. During an icy cold winter, Isabel arranged to join her in Chicago for a day of book promotion. They'd be staying overnight and within walking distance of Michael Reese Psychiatric Hospital, where Isabel's mother had been a patient for the last ten years.

It was comically disorienting each time Isabel tried phoning her mother in the hospital. With the kind of determination one couldn't help but admire, a patient had managed to hang himself with a phone cord. As a precaution, the hospital installed the only available phone in plain sight; and in the institution's misguided attempt to normalize the appearance of its obviously abnormal boarding community, patients were encouraged to answer any incoming call. Each time Isabel tried phoning her mother, another disenfranchised voice interceded. It would either rush her through a paranoid monologue or, in slurred and overmedicated droning, lull her into a soporific trance. Every patient answering Isabel's calls took the opportunity to tell his or her own story.

Had she not traveled to Chicago while her father was out of

town; had the publicist not booked her into the author's favorite Chicago hotel; had that hotel not been within walking distance to the hospital, Isabel never would have heard her mother's story. It all fit together as if preordained. There was only one remaining piece of information required for the jigsaw puzzle to take shape.

Miss Drake maintained a consistently formal relationship with Mr. Simpson during her thirty loyal years as his secretary. Among her many duties was to draft checks for his personal bills, including those made out to his wife's psychiatrist. After keeping Mrs. Simpson's condition a secret for her entire career, Miss Drake responded to Isabel's inquiry with the relief of someone who had waited a very long time before finally allowing herself to be unburdened of the information.

"Yes, I can provide the name of your mother's doctor," said Miss Drake.

Her cooperation was so unexpected, Isabel stood motionless: one hand holding the receiver, the other unprepared to react even though it was holding a pen. By the time Isabel understood she'd been offered the doctor's phone number, she wasn't entirely sure she had transcribed it accurately. She dared not ask Miss Drake to repeat it. Looking down at the seven numbers scrawled quickly on the hotel's phone pad, Isabel realized she had grouped the numbers together like the combination to a locked safe.

With the doctor's name, but without any knowledge of the person to whom it belonged, Isabel placed her call.

"Dr. Stutz, this is Tisza Simpson's daughter. I'm in from New York, and was hoping you might be willing to see me."

"I won't compromise my doctor-patient relationship," was the doctor's rote reply.

"I understand," said Isabel, sounding disappointed.

"I can give you basic information about her illness," the doctor volunteered.

"Fine," Isabel agreed.

"Come by my office after rounds tonight, say, about ten o'clock."

Isabel found Dr. Stutz's office by walking toward the one light in an otherwise deserted hospital hall. The doctor, engrossed in paperwork, left the door ajar in anticipation of her visit. Shaking his hand as he half rose to greet her, Isabel's first impression was that everything about him looked tired.

"Please, take a seat." He motioned as he sat back down.

Now it begins, thought Isabel. His first words will speak for whatever follows.

"Nothing can be done about your mother's mental illness. Not now. Not ever," was the doctor's preamble. "I understand you found her the day she tried to kill herself," he said.

Isabel didn't answer.

Dr. Stutz explained aloofly that her mother's "case" had been reviewed by countless doctors and ultimately reduced to the chemical craft of balancing medications so that Mrs. Simpson might have what he referred to as "acceptable days." Isabel wondered how he defined an acceptable day, but decided not to ask.

Isabel also wondered whether the doctor possessed any more detail of her mother's murky past than she'd managed to find out on her own. The only concrete information Isabel was ever able to ascertain was that, like her father, her mother had no living relatives. I don't even know where she came from, Isabel thought while listening to Dr. Stutz's prognosis. She looked for signs he might be holding on to more information than he was volunteering. He didn't seem to be.

10

Mrs. Simpson spoke a number of languages: German to Vera; French to her dressmaker; and Italian to the butcher.

"How did you come to America?" Isabel asked her mother, but not until she was an adult herself.

"I came from Vienna to pursue my music," her mother responded obliquely, with a reference to motive but none to logistics.

"Where? And how old were you?" Isabel asked.

"Juilliard. In New York. Which is where I met your father. I played the piano." The concise response answered three separate questions and at the same time raised another — completely unexpected — one.

"But we never had a piano in the house."

"Deliberately."

"Why?"

"Because I knew."

"Knew what?"

"How it was meant to be played . . . how it should have sounded."

"What does that matter?" Isabel asked.

"It's all that matters," her mother said with more emotion

than she was usually willing to extend. "My hands were injured when I was a little girl. I could play only so well."

"How did you injure your hands?"

Isabel waited for her mother to explain. Mrs. Simpson stood up. "Please excuse me, won't you?"

Isabel could remember only one other anecdote from her mother's personal history. When Ian was a young boy, he asked why he and his sister had light complexions when hers was so dark.

"When I was your age, Ian, I spent the summers in a very small Hungarian village," began Mrs. Simpson. The introductory line held the promise of her long-awaited tale.

". . . A village so small that the baker was also the town crier." She had the children's rapt attention. "And when the gypsies camped in the hills on the outskirts of the town, the baker would close his shop in order to warn the townspeople. He would walk up and down the narrow cobblestone streets ringing a large bell."

Ian asked his mother why the gypsies were viewed with such suspicion. Mrs. Simpson stared at her son as though he should have known.

"The gypsies stole fair-haired children," was all she said.

The children assumed the gypsies were a sidebar and that there would be more to the story. They waited respectfully for their mother to resume. But there would be no more story. Instead, she suggested they go to bed.

"You shouldn't have asked her about the gypsies," snapped Isabel as they were climbing the steps to their rooms. "What difference could that have possibly made when we were so close to something more important?"

"But Izzie, maybe Mother was what they call a 'changeling,'

and when the gypsies stole a blond child from the village, they replaced it with a dark one who was Mother."

Isabel dismissed the idea. "Don't be absurd."

Isabel knew her brother to be a sweet boy, but his naïveté was inconvenient at times, and it had just derailed what she thought would be a crucial chance at some real information.

"It wasn't a trade arrangement. They just stole the blond ones and kept their own," she explained impatiently, then added, "gypsies are a tribe. They would never be separated from one another."

Ian reflected on her last comment as they lingered at the top of the stairs.

"And so even though they didn't have homes, they'd always stay together," he added to her pronouncement. "Izzie, what is our family exactly?"

"I have no idea, Ian, but whatever we are, it's the opposite of a tribe."

The aborted tale provided no explanation of the difference in complexions between Mrs. Simpson and her children. But, by placing her in an identified country in Eastern Europe, it offered a small geographical detail from her own childhood, assuming any part was true. . . .

Assuming any part of it was true, the gypsies were the least of it. Isabel was wrong about how much the doctor knew. With a voluminous file marked "Simpson" in the middle of his desk, Dr. Stutz relayed what Isabel had never expected to hear from anyone. He told it in words that were dry as sand because the slightest embellishment in its narration would have made her mother's story unbelievable.

11

Isabel was more unusual-looking than beautiful.

Years of enforced ballet had imposed a formidable bearing some mistook as imperiousness. Isabel's greatest weakness was an often sudden and sometimes violent temper. When she felt it building, Isabel would try to control her temper by forging it into words as sharp as surgical instruments. But there were times Isabel's temper would not provide advance notice to the rest of her being, and it would strike with a dangerous voltage.

Isabel was instinctively feminine, but she felt sure she understood men. She knew them to be less apologetic about their needs than were women. With the exception of her brother, she had rarely witnessed male vulnerability. What she couldn't help but notice was their specific kind of obliviousness. It often exposed anyone who happened to be in its path — women and children especially — to hurt.

Despite her cautious view of them, Isabel grew up very much liking men. As a woman, she especially liked men when they conducted themselves as gentlemen — and at times, in the confines of the bedroom, when they did not. Never did she believe that men were meant to provide whatever she wanted but couldn't have on her own. Lovers added to Isabel in infinitely different ways. Some sharpened her intellect, others sated her sexual appetite, but none had claimed her heart.

Because Isabel moved in predominantly male circles, she kept a distance between herself and her professional associates. John Vance was the exception. There were three people Isabel trusted with her life: Ian, Monina, and John.

John was twice her age and published books under his own imprint within her company. He lived in San Francisco and scheduled trips to New York every season. During his trip in the spring, Isabel invited him to stay the weekend at her rented cottage in Connecticut. They'd be able to decide on John's next publishing list without the distractions of the office. As a young single woman reporting to older conservative businessmen, Isabel knew to conduct her private life with discretion. "Appear like Caesar's wife — above reproach," her father advised. John was gay, and there would be no suggestion of impropriety in his overnight stay.

A familiar figure in the publishing industry, John had built a reputation by acquiring and editing autobiographies of famous — and infamous — actors, rock stars, and, most recently, ex-presidents. Isabel never asked after John's personal life. She knew only that he had been married to a movie actress, and that he was a valued member of the cognoscenti. But there was more to John than ampersands. Resorting to drugs and alcohol after his wife died, he had the centered soul of a man who managed to face down his demons without losing any part of his generous sense of humor.

"They dry-cleaned me at Hazelden," John said, his eyes sparkling with mischief, when he introduced himself to Isabel. "And now I'm ready to work again."

No one else but Isabel would hire him. She bestowed complete faith by offering John an imprint. He thanked her by producing one best seller after another.

Their country weekend unfolded without any unusual note until shortly before they returned to the city. A single, arbitrary occurrence that Sunday afternoon set in motion events that would change Isabel's life.

As Isabel waited for John to finish the section in the Sunday *New York Times* she had yet to see, she reached for a part of the paper she probably wouldn't have looked at otherwise. Her eyes scanned the Travel section. Not expecting to find anything of interest, they came to rest on a particular article, which she read with great care.

Words led Isabel to James. How could it have been otherwise?

Words drew Isabel to James and, in time, to a place she couldn't have imagined. His words would hold her there, long after she should have left. They would provoke her blind rage . . . and become reason enough for Isabel to try killing him.

12

James Willoughby came from a family that included a "signer."

For those not familiar with the expression, James's mother would be quick to explain that a Willoughby ancestor signed the Declaration of Independence. The various Willoughby trust funds, once presumed limitless, dwindled to a trickle before James was born. He grew up in frayed-cuff gentility living on the only remaining family asset — an estate in Virginia. The rambling house had its own floating heaviness. A dank smell of the past permeated its rooms. Willoughbys believed that they were cut from slightly better material than the rest. They convinced themselves that ancestral distinction compensated for the rotting windowsills and flaking paint.

It could be accurately said that without Willoughbys, there would have been no Simpsons. Seventeenth-century English shipping was responsible for what had been the Willoughby fortune, and it was a Willoughby trading ship that had facilitated the expulsion of the Simpson brothers from London.

Willoughby holdings increased with an eighteenth-century land grant. The Willoughby township included a town of Willoughby. Willoughby ambition was rewarded by abundant wealth; but subsequent generations of the great family became mired in inertia. Entitlement replaced motivation. Virtually everything removable had long been sold: first the important paintings; then the valuable furniture; and last, the rare bibelots. The only thing left was the land — every acre of the original twelve hundred. Untouched by agricultural initiatives, the vast property remained a natural wilderness. In all of his travels as an adult, James would see no more beautiful a place than the setting he had as a child.

Willoughbys never questioned their own tradition. They were *les bienseances,* which, if forced from French into English, describes "the always-have-beens." Each generation rotated the three Willoughby male names: George, William, and James. All of them lived off reminiscences of their predecessors until the dividends began to slow down. Eventually, the checks stopped arriving altogether. It was then that the Willoughbys broke a cardinal rule of independent wealth: they began to live off their principal. When that was entirely depleted, they waited for dead relatives to bequeath just enough to bridge them to the next modest iterance of inheritance.

By the time George Willoughby — James's father — graduated from Princeton, there were no more relatives left to die. Not even secondary ones. George was compelled to take the only action he believed available. He married for money. Or so he thought. George Willoughby made the mistake of confusing pedigree with cash flow. With a little more due diligence, he might have unearthed the fact that his affianced was equally impoverished. Each assumed the other would be bringing the money.

Neither knew their predicament until the morning after the wedding night. Upon discovering his miscalculation, George

Willoughby poured himself a drink before breakfast. The newly christened Mrs. George Willoughby — realizing there was no way out for either of them — offered the only solace she could think of: "George, my family has lost its fortune, but it has held on to something of greater value . . . an unsullied background."

James didn't talk as an infant. He would point. When he wanted something to eat, he would point to the object and then to his mouth. If something caught his eye, he would point to the object and point to the person with whom he wished to share his interest. The pediatrician pronounced James to be both physically and mentally sound.

Mrs. Willoughby was sure her son would come to language in his own time. Whenever he pointed to an object, she would patiently name the word. This went on for years without any indication that James would ever speak. One night during a walk after supper, he pointed upward and looked at his mother before pointing upward again.

"Yes, James, that is the night sky," his mother said with determination.

He pointed again.

"Perhaps you mean the trees," she corrected herself.

"Aren't the trees beautiful against the night sky?" she added with an emphasis on *the night sky.*

James offered his first verbal communication in a complete sentence, without its flow slowing between words: "The night is only the black around the stars," he said, finally. As James's mother stared at him in disbelief, he added, "I close my eyes and I can still see them."

By the time James was born, the family had been in hock for two generations. Everyone in the town of Willoughby — no matter how modest their means — had more financial wherewithal than the Willoughbys themselves. It was no secret that Willoughby checks had a nasty habit of bouncing. Even though George stiffed the Social Register Association for its annual dues, the Black Book continued to list his family.

The Willoughbys lived within the very narrow compass that was their township. James attended the local public grade school, where he was considered flamboyantly odd. Yearning for adventure, James cloistered himself in the house's large attic, poring over well-worn foreign periodicals . . . none of which were published later than the nineteenth century, when the Willoughby money dried up.

During his countless hours in the attic, James came across family photo albums that had recorded various ancestral journeys to Europe. The last of the photos halted in mid-book. Staring out at James were his great-grandparents, photographed during their tour of Naples. The Naples photos led James to the public library, where he read, first, Goethe's *Italian Journey*, next Henry James's *Italian Hours* and D. H. Lawrence's *Twilight in Italy*, and then Norman Douglas's *Life in Capri* and Elio Vittorini's *Conversations in Sicily*.

And so it began. Working his way through all of the albums, James visited every foreign country the albums pictured by whatever could be read in books.

With each passing year, James felt his world becoming more and more claustrophobic. On a clear afternoon, looking up from a back issue of *Holiday* magazine and gazing out the window of the Willoughby public library, James was completely sure of one thing: whatever interested him could no longer be found where he was sitting.

James was the only remaining namesake to the Willoughby

dynasty. His lineage could be charted in one long, straight channel back to its origin. But what James Whickham Braxton Willoughby didn't have was the first clue on how to make his way forward in a world that, less and less, recognized any relevance in his bloodlines.

America counts itself a nation of achievers. Men are expected to be industrious and women resourceful. Mrs. Willoughby lived up to that expectation; her husband unapologetically did not. George Willoughby managed to keep himself busy designing and redesigning the estate's various gardens while his wife managed a formidably large house. She admitted to no one that hers was a household without servants. Tirelessly, she did herself whatever was required to keep that truth from plain sight.

Having given up on her husband long ago, Mrs. Willoughby was devoted to her son. She loved James with the determination of a woman who believed that, by molding him into the ideal man, she would rectify her disappointment in his entire gender. James knew that it was just a question of time before his mother would consume him. At fourteen, he told his parents he wanted to go away to school.

Just as they had at Princeton, Willoughby ancestors bequeathed funds for their direct descendants at Andover. James was obliged to supplement his scholarship with mandatory duties. Sunday evenings included the formality of a sit-down dinner. Along with the other scholarship students, James was expected to serve the full-paying ones. Determined to erase the taint of this weekly humiliation, James excelled academically. Andover provided the means to advance James's natural gift for writing.

James was naturally endowed with another gift: charm. He made himself well liked, especially among women. Andover —

with Exeter and Groton in its immediate neighborhood — granted James his first real look at serious wealth. During school vacations, he was invited to houses in Greenwich and Bedford. Summers were spent with his friends' families in Newport or on Fisher Island.

James's impeccable manners made him a favorite among his schoolmates' mothers. By the time he left Andover, James had become a seasoned houseguest. He also had become quite used to the amenities of wealth.

Princeton received James without question, just as it had his father. Graduating with honors, James had the advantages of education, background, social connections, and extreme good looks. James never questioned any of these advantages; he took them for granted. The only question needing an answer was just how James would take advantage of his advantages.

Browsing through what was left of the family library, James had stumbled upon a book that made a lasting impression: *Society as I Have Found It*. Narrated in the first person by Ward McAllister, it detailed the leisure class in America's nineteenth century. James thought the author to be absurdly self-important, but there was nothing absurd about the world of aesthetic pleasure and personal pursuits he described. It was exactly what James wanted for himself.

The unwelcome circumstance that presented itself to James after college was the need to earn a living. He decided upon a means of support that looked less like work and more like the moneyed environs to which he had gravitated. James picked a niche and wrote about something very few had, but everyone else wanted a vicarious glimpse of. He wrote about members of a social stratum whose money allowed them unfettered time, and whose lives regularly included travel to the most perfect meal in Paris and the most luxurious hotel suite in London.

James's successful writing career was a self-fulfilling cycle. He acknowledged the rich with tasteful wit. They reciprocated with invitations. James was able to participate in a way of life to which he aspired without admitting his pursuit of it.

13

Isabel's eye, which had been scanning the page, was drawn to it immediately.

Unconventional and beautifully written, James's article in the Sunday *New York Times* was about his childhood home. It seemed an odd bit of writing for the Travel section. The fact was, James didn't deliver the article on St. Bart he'd been assigned. He'd taken the trip, enjoyed the beaches and hotels, but had no real interest in writing about it. James handed in a personal essay instead. The writing was so winning, the editor of the Travel section ran it despite its subject.

Isabel looked up, having read it twice, and asked John, "Are you familiar with a writer by the name of James Willoughby?"

There was a long silence before John answered, "I know him well."

"Take a look at this," Isabel said as she handed the paper over to John, who was draped over the sofa.

Isabel left the room and returned with a pot of tea. Setting a tray on the ottoman in front of him, she waited to hear John's opinion. John finished reading and pushed his glasses above his eyebrows so that they rested on his forehead.

"It's remarkably good writing. I'm not surprised. And he's a unique personality."

"Why don't we approach him to write outside his field?" suggested Isabel.

"Because he's impossible to work with."

"How do you know?"

"Darling, I just do. Trust me on this. He's impossible."

"But they all are in one way or another; it's just a question of degree. That's the deal: whoever has the talent gets to be impossible . . . and whoever spots the talent gets the privilege of being a little nearer to it than the rest. This kind of writing is worth the trouble of its author. He writes about being a child in the best way possible . . . it reminds me of Lawrence Durrell's brother, Gerald. Have you ever read *My Family and Other Animals*?"

"No," John answered curtly.

"It's an absolutely magical autobiography of his boyhood on Corfu. He wrote it with all the sophistication of his adult talent, but — here's the thing — he was able to tell us, to remind us, what was important as a child."

"I'll make a point of reading it," muttered John.

"John, *my* point is, it's rare to find this particular gift among even the really good writers. *My* point is that we're in the business of working with writers. So *my* point is, why not at least approach him?"

John was becoming annoyed. Isabel was pushing, and he didn't like it. Not over this. Not over something he knew would be a mistake.

"I'll arrange an introduction, but that's it. I won't publish him. If you want to take on Willoughby, you'll have to do it outside of my imprint."

Isabel persisted.

"Where is he from?"

"Virginia," said John.

There was an awkward silence. Realizing he'd not explained what must have sounded to Isabel like an uncompromising position, John sat up on the couch, poured his tea, and in his familiarly mellow but wicked tone, proceeded to regale her with what he knew of James Willoughby.

"He comes from blue blood. You know what I say about blue blood? Blue blood is tired blood. I think there's a township called Willoughby. Acres of land and a beautiful eighteenth-century estate. I remember his fortieth birthday party there. The guests were very grand, and it was all a great deal of fun, but the setting was like something out of *Cold Comfort Farm*. The father wandered the grounds wearing a threadbare smoking jacket. The mother is stunning in a Nancy Mitford kind of way . . . but something in life must have disappointed her, and she's holding all of that resentment around her mouth. They're tremendous snobs with deliberate elocution and the most beautiful cutlery — probably the last thing that hasn't been sold yet to pay the taxes. With the exception of James, who's quite a dresser, the lot of them looked a bit dingy, as though they'd given up separating their whites from their colored clothes before doing the laundry. James married — and then divorced quickly. Who knows what the story was there . . ."

Isabel listened with great enjoyment, but she was not deterred.

"So where can we find him? He can't still be living in his childhood home."

"Don't be so sure. But no . . . I think he has an apartment in New York. And yes, I'll track him down if that's what you really want. But, Isabel, please promise you'll think about it before doing anything. With all due respect to the fact you pay my salary, you're too young to have any common sense. I've logged in enough experience to be able to see trouble walking toward me. The last thing you do is cross the street to invite it to lunch."

"Invite it to lunch," said Isabel.

14

With nothing riding on the call but the obligation to set a lunch date, John phoned James's agent, Rebecca Gibbs.

"Does she understand how impossible he is?" was Rebecca's first question. "I can barely find anyone to work with Willoughby and two thousand words. No one could survive him through the completion of a book."

"I've warned her —"

"Isabel needs a few more years of experience to temper her judgment," said Rebecca. "I have Dior hanging in my closet older than she is."

"I don't know," said John. "All experience has managed to do with most of us is drain away our optimism."

"I suppose you're right," replied Rebecca after brief reflection. "I'm the first to admit to cosmic fatigue."

"Maybe Isabel will convince James to take himself seriously," John suggested.

He didn't believe a word of it.

Neither did Rebecca. She dismissed John's remark and James's literary potential in the same comment: "What a completely ridiculous thing to say."

Rebecca was far more interested in an answer to her next question.

"Does Isabel know what James looks like?"

"He could look like Quasimodo for all she cares," replied John.

"So she hasn't seen just how lethally attractive he is, and she hasn't heard about his behavior toward women?"

John chuckled. "Okay . . . *now* I get it."

Rebecca Gibbs was a highly reputable agent who had long ago given up trying to advance James's career. She continued to represent him for the strategic reason that he knew almost everyone. If James was inexcusable — which was becoming more and more the case when he was egged on by drinking — she thought of him as something she was forced to endure professionally for the sake of extending her social reach. But even when he didn't drink, there were two things about James that galled Rebecca: his entitlement and his louche way with women.

"A man far too dependent on women to power himself through life," is how she once described James before prudence could catch her words.

Regardless of what she thought of him personally, James was Rebecca's client. She knew it would be unprofessional to participate in the disrespectful exchange under way. On the other hand, there was nothing wrong with enjoying John's wry sense of humor over morning coffee. She would listen — but not contribute — to the conversation.

"Our own Isabel doesn't know what he looks like," John repeated. Without any reaction from Rebecca, he continued, "But Becky, what's far more interesting is the fact he doesn't know what *she* looks like. . . . And I get to be there when he does," he added gleefully.

John began to sketch the scene. "Just think about it, darling.

Take one brief but blissful moment out of what I'm sure will be a relentlessly busy morning and think about it."

Still no response.

"Becky . . . ? Becky, I know you're listening, and I'm sure you're smiling."

Indeed she was. For very similar reasons, they were both savoring an imagined meeting between Isabel and James.

"As soon as he sees what he's stumbled into, that male need to conquer will shift into overdrive."

John paused for the sake of theatrics.

"He won't pay the slightest attention to the opportunity she's offering. I can visualize it now. Becky, I want you to visualize it with me, because I know exactly what will happen."

Undaunted by Rebecca's refusal to join in, John continued his running monologue. "I've seen it before . . . when Isabel senses she's not being taken seriously, she goes as silent as a submarine turning off its engine. What was that movie . . . *Run Silent, Run Deep* . . . Darling, what was that movie called?"

Thoroughly entertained but not giving John any indication of it, Rebecca answered in a deliberate monotone, "I don't know, John. I can't say."

"It was set in World War II. . . . I'm sure that was its name. The entire movie took place under water during the course of an extremely tense situation . . . an American submarine forced to drift silently on the ocean floor because a Japanese ship was stalking it from above . . . men with chiseled good looks in a confined space on our side, and subtitles on theirs," John enthused.

John was on a roll. Rebecca put her hand over the receiver so he wouldn't hear her laughter while he continued.

"The point is, James will be utterly oblivious — you know how self-involved he is — he'll just continue to push the charm.

61

Isabel will low-crawl on the bottom of the ocean, maneuvering around his advances as though they were depth charges. She'll send out a faint signal, allowing him to know she's still down there . . . encouraging him to believe she's not entirely unavailable. Then, just at the moment he thinks he's gotten by with something, she'll break radio silence and surface."

Sounding like the last few lines in a cautionary tale, John warned, "You know Isabel's temper. Mark my words, Miss Rebecca, it will be swift and cruel. He won't have the slightest idea until he tries to get up from the lunch table and realizes there's nothing where his legs once were. She'll just leave him there, bobbing in the water like a cork."

"Have fun for the both of us," Rebecca said before she took another call.

15

John chose Orso, a fashionable restaurant with an arty clientele, for the backdrop to what he was sure would be a memorable lunch.

As he held the door open for Isabel, John spotted James inside. He was walking toward them. John assumed James's intention was to greet them as they entered. Isabel, rummaging through her purse, stepped into the restaurant at the exact time James was leaving it. Looking from her purse downward, what she noticed first were the shoes: handmade Belgian loafers in rich brown suede with lime green piping. Walking straight into their owner, she looked up at a tall, raffish man whose reddish brown hair was combed back off a patrician face. His eyes, the color of pale blue marbles, met hers only for a split second before he continued his forward motion out the door . . . without so much as a hello.

"I've made every crummy deal of my life in this restaurant. Let's eat somewhere else," was all James said on his way past his two hosts.

The restaurant reservation had been made in Isabel's name. What was originally to be a business meeting seemed to have become a situation — one that threw Isabel off her mark. There she was, unexpectedly left standing on the sidewalk in front of Orso, feeling unhinged. Isabel decided to start again from the beginning. She was about to introduce herself properly when James turned away, either ignoring or not seeing her outstretched hand. He was striding across the street before anything could be said or done.

Isabel was baffled. "Can you believe this?" she asked John.

"I warned you. What did I say about crossing the street to invite trouble to lunch?"

"What do we do — follow him?"

"Traffic getting here was awful — we might as well stay," suggested John. "I'll call Orso and apologize once we're back in the office."

James had already disappeared into an unfamiliar restaurant on the other side of the street.

"Who the hell does he think he is, and where the hell is he taking us?" Isabel asked John as they dodged oncoming cars to catch up with James.

"He certainly knows who he is — that's never been his problem," said John. "And apparently he knows where he's going, so that's not an issue for him either."

"Why insist on another restaurant?"

"I have absolutely no idea."

"It's a display of territorial imperative," said Isabel.

"You're right . . . he's marking his trees. But think of the dreary budget meeting waiting for us back at the office. In another few hours you'll be grateful for some excitement to your day."

"Are you suggesting there's a kind of lyrical spontaneity to his rudeness?" Isabel snipped. "Is he always this arrogant?"

"Always," was all John had a chance to say before they stepped into the restaurant of James's choosing. He had commandeered a table and was standing behind the chair already pulled out for Isabel.

"We've yet to have the opportunity of introducing ourselves," Isabel said before allowing James to seat her. She held out her hand so that, this time, it couldn't be ignored. "Isabel Simpson." Without affectation, James bowed ever so slightly. The gesture seemed as natural as his pulling out her chair. Isabel hadn't seen that kind of gallantry since her childhood. Despite an unwillingness to admit it, she had already begun to forgive James for his restaurant switch.

After James seated Isabel, he turned to John.

"John, how good of you to arrange this introduction."

Her lunch meeting would now assume the semblance of something constructive, thought Isabel. She could finally get down to business.

"So tell me," James said, looking only at John. "What's become of Veronique?"

Isabel had no idea who Veronique was. As soon as she saw John's uncomfortable reaction, she realized the woman must have been a onetime paramour of James's. Instead of observing polite discourse, James hijacked the conversation.

"She left San Francisco several years ago," said John. He hoped a pithy answer might discourage James from continuing the inappropriate trajectory.

"I heard she married a rich Jew," was James's stunning next comment.

It was as though, rather than being spoken, the unpredicted statement had fallen from the ceiling. Weighted by impossibly heavy implication, its descent was so sudden that it created a vacuum where previously there had been conversation. Isabel put down her menu and waited for another qualifying sentence from James. She was sure something — some add-on — was forthcoming.

"But we should order," was all James said as he signaled the waitress.

Isabel looked over to John, who was shielding his face with a menu. She turned from the menu-shielded John and, holding on to her incredulity from the moment before, looked expectantly at James, who, much to her relief, returned her look.

"What would you like to eat, my dear?" was all he offered.

The reference to "my dear" struck Isabel as patronizing given the purpose of the lunch. But protocol was dwarfed by larger questions. In the wake of his highly provocative description of Veronique's choice of husbands, Isabel felt as if she'd been dropshipped into treacherously unfamiliar territory. There was such a dramatic disconnect between what Isabel thought she had heard James say and the comfort with which he appeared to have said it, she was sure some part of it wasn't registering. Was there a fleeting — but crucial — word not heard, whose absence hurled her into an unintended textual interpretation? Or perhaps she hadn't been able to see around the blind curve of a misplaced modifier . . .

James appeared to be at least fifteen years older than Isabel. Despite his erratic behavior, he possessed the manners of a gentleman. Maybe it was a generational issue of semantics, thought Isabel, and James meant no disrespect. This was, after all, New York City. Willoughby was a sophisticate. If he were anti-Semitic, surely he wouldn't be parading it in the middle of the theater district.

Everything about it was so unlikely, Isabel came to the conclusion she must have misunderstood. That was it . . . she'd simply misconstrued James's comment. What's more, he was acting as though he was more host than guest. Yes, now she had it. James was recklessly flippant and undoubtedly a snob, but he wasn't a bigot.

Once Isabel convinced herself she hadn't heard what she'd actually heard, she was equally sure James was taking them to lunch . . . particularly since he had just ordered a bottle of Dom Perignon.

"I'll have the lentil salad, thank you," she said. "You're very kind to order the champagne. But I've scheduled a budget meeting for this afternoon that will call on all of my wits. I'd like an iced tea, if you please."

"Pity . . . A budget meeting, you say. I can't imagine," said James.

Isabel was trying very hard not to presuppose this last comment wasn't another mark of condescension. Perhaps he meant he couldn't imagine a budget meeting per se, not that he couldn't imagine her overseeing one.

The waitress — who Isabel placed in her mid-twenties — uncorked the most expensive bottle of champagne on the wine list. Isabel noticed James's eye exchange with her. John was busy laying conversational groundwork for the book proposal and wasn't watching the subtle pas de deux. Isabel was. She got it right away. James was having a fling with the waitress. He'd switched their lunch location in order to enjoy himself at everyone else's inconvenience. He never had any intention of taking either Isabel — or her book proposal — seriously.

Isabel was so astonished by the range of James's unacceptable behavior, she was no longer certain about her earlier evaluation of the man as a possible anti-Semite. But she was sure of two things:

during the past fifteen minutes, John had been speaking to James's deaf ears; and the food, which had just arrived, wouldn't be the only thing the waitress would be serving James that afternoon.

When the lentil salad was placed in front of Isabel, James observed, "You're being very quiet, Madam Publisher."

If ever there were a sound of impending calamity, it resonated in those words.

16

As John had predicted in his phone conversation with Rebecca, Isabel went silent as soon as she knew that she was not being taken seriously.

She turned off her engines, drifted down to the bottom of the ocean, tuned out all exterior stimuli, and began to create a mental inventory of issues to be reviewed during the third-quarter financial meeting scheduled with her staff that afternoon. Isabel's concentration was interrupted when James excused himself from the table. He planned his trip to the men's room to coincide with the arrival of the bill. When Isabel realized James never had any intention of paying for their lunch or the champagne he drank entirely on his own, her face registered disbelief for the last time that afternoon.

John wasn't the least surprised at James's affrontery. It was a predictable conclusion to any encounter with James Willoughby. Someone always ended up picking up his tab. The moment of reckoning had arrived. It lay in that final catalytic instant Isabel understood just how far she had been led astray. For the split second it flickered, John saw her murderous look. Then a veil of calm descended over Isabel, and she gave the waitress a credit card.

That's it, thought John, she's breaking radio silence. He

looked up and saw James returning to the table. John looked over to Isabel. She had emerged from the ocean floor and was sighting her target. James sat down. He was now in Isabel's crosshairs. The poor bastard has no idea, thought John.

Deliberately catching James's attention so she could look straight at him as she discharged her first torpedo, Isabel said politely, "Mr. Willoughby, your shoes are the most impressive thing about you."

James's face searched for an expression.

"Like you, they have decoratively thin soles," continued Isabel in a voice that sounded no alarm. "The next time around, you and your shoes might fare better at another table . . . with someone else. Someone you'd have more of a chance impressing with your empty virtuosity."

Isabel turned to John.

"John, you'll forgive me for wasting your time, won't you? It was my mistake to expect something more from Mr. Willoughby."

Isabel placed her napkin on the table. It was her sign to John that they were leaving as soon as the bill was paid. She turned back to James and stared right through him, taking her eyes off of his nonplussed face long enough to sign the credit card receipt.

With a look John later described to Rebecca as "something that could freeze hell," Isabel detonated the second warhead . . .

"I've not included a gratuity. I assume you'll provide one when the young lady goes off duty . . . or do you have a barter arrangement with her?"

Not for a moment during the attack did Isabel appear the least bit upset. Even when speaking invectives, her manner gave no indication of their acidity.

James didn't know what had hit him.

Isabel's dismissal was like a blinding blow to the head; her lacerating rebuke, like flying shrapnel. Bruised and bloodied, James looked up from his sitting position. . . . Isabel was gone before he could collect his wits.

When they returned to the office, John made two calls before heading into the budget meeting. One was an apology to the manager of Orso for reserving a good table and not showing up; the other was to Rebecca.

"Darling, I can't talk now, but you'll need to phone Isabel and make amends for your client."

"How bad was it?"

"Better than the worst that you could have ever imagined."

17

There were very few times that James was left sitting as a woman stood.

"What the hell was that all about?" James asked out loud as he watched Isabel leave. Something nasty had just happened, James was sure; but it happened so suddenly, it was impossible to identify. Isabel's departure — orchestrated on her own terms — not only prevented James from defending himself, it denied him the dignity of getting to his feet. Insult had been added to injury; and James was left just sitting there, feeling foolish in a way that couldn't be repaired.

"What the hell *was* that all about?" repeated James, as if taking his own pulse. *She came at me with absolutely no warning. Not even a shot across the bow. Damned if I know what set her off. She's obviously disturbed in a dangerously random way.*

Further reflection forced James to admit there had been nothing random about Isabel's behavior — quite the opposite. Her timing was as precise as a stopwatch. And the calm delivery was like a kick pleat to that infuriating confidence of hers. She'd made a point of looking right through him as she inflicted not one, but two insults that were now deeply lodged in his male pride.

"We'll have today's dessert tomorrow," James said to the waitress.

"Just what kind of woman was *that*?" she demanded to know.

"One who tries to pee standing up," was his sarcastic reply.

Needing to believe it more than he did, James knew what he had said was probably not true. Who was this woman, indeed? She was not as he had pictured. He'd imagined a dowdy, older woman married to work. This one was too young for someone with her kind of professional standing; and she had a bearing that managed to dislodge his own. That tongue of hers could clip a hedge, thought James. He wasn't sure if he was more humiliated by Isabel's verbal brinkmanship or by not having seen the possibility of it beneath the camouflage of ladylike demeanor.

James was at a loss. Rarely had anyone taken a position against him. Certainly not a woman. James had never been required to explain himself because he was what everyone wanted . . . a social-registered, Ivy Leagued, handsomely mannered man in fine tailoring who'd been awarded membership to life's elite club by just showing up.

James had a taste for the unfinished, and didn't always have plans from one day to the next. He accepted work only if it were financially necessary or intellectually appealing. It was the former of the two circumstances that had brought him to the lunch table that day.

James arrived at Orso with a hangover from the night before. He'd gone to something or another. Had it been Aids Research or the Brooklyn Zoo? He couldn't remember. He left with a woman seated at his table . . . he could barely remember her either. James returned home the next morning in his tuxedo. Before showering, he made a potion from Brazilian *quarana* to combat a hangover, looked at his calendar, and realized that it was the day his agent had committed him to a lunch meeting with a book publisher. Jesus, James thought to himself. Goddamn Rebecca.

She had called a week ago.

"James, are you sober and alert?"

"Though one requires attendance on the other, Rebecca dear, I am not often both."

"Well, try paying attention because there may be money in it."

"Really?" said James with newfound interest.

"Do you remember John Vance?"

"With great fondness."

"He has his own imprint at Priam Books. I gather his publisher read your piece in the *Times* and asked John to track you down."

"Like a mad dog?"

"How do you mean?"

"Track me down, like a mad dog."

"Please don't start — I don't have time."

"Just a little levity . . . you really should make time. It might put things in perspective."

"James, are you interested or not?"

"I'm always interested in anyone willing to part with their money. A book publisher, you say? A book could bring more income than several years of magazine articles."

"All right, I'll tell John to make the arrangements. Lunch will be you, John, and the publisher. I'll loop back if you're all in agreement."

"Why don't I just agree now?" asked James. "For the record, I'm in complete agreement with whatever will add to my bank account."

"James."

"My dear?"

"You don't seem to understand."

"What am I not understanding? I'm interested."

"What you're not understanding is that they have to be interested in you as well."

"Of course they're interested. What could possibly be the point of their lunch invitation if they weren't?"

Before Rebecca had a chance to spell it out, James added, "What's important is my own degree of interest. And they happen to come calling when it's extremely high."

"James."

"Yes?"

"I know it's difficult for you to comprehend, but there's more than your own willingness at issue."

"I can't imagine."

"Try."

"All right."

"Yes, and?"

"I meant, all right, I've tried, and I can't imagine an issue beyond my own degree of interest."

"What about the issue of whether they think they can work with you? It's their idea, after all."

"What do you mean, the lunch?"

"I mean *the book*. They have a book idea, James."

"They're publishers. Publishers don't have ideas."

"Well, this one has."

"That's bloody presumptuous of him."

"For God's sake . . . James, do you want to hear them out or not?"

"Okay, okay —"

"One last thing. The publisher is not a man. The publisher is a woman. Please don't force me to apologize to her afterward."

"A woman? You can't be serious."

"Yes, a woman."

"I'll be damned. Are you sure?"

"Go see for yourself."

18

James had always chafed at the word *money.*

For James, money never had added, only subtracted . . . depleting his mother, degrading his father, hovering like a specter and inciting bitter arguments between them. Because James rarely saw it handled as a child, money remained an abstraction to him as an adult. He would often say money "annoyed" him. James was annoyed that — unlike the well-heeled people about whom he wrote who presumed money and rarely discussed it — he had to find the means of earning it.

The day before James received Rebecca's call, he'd just returned from a month in Europe accompanying an American heiress, recently divorced and even more recently diagnosed with advanced cancer. It would be one last trip before hers to the grave; and she was determined to spend as much money as humanly possible along the way.

James exhausted his bank account by tipping the armies of support staff required at each of the Ritz hotels connecting their travel, like dots, from one foreign city to the next. On their return to New York via London, the ATM on Upper Brook Street rejected James's relatively modest request and — in no uncertain terms — reminded him what he'd be coming home to. Two black-ink words printed on the discreetly small withdrawal receipt conveyed unhappy information: "Insufficient Funds."

James was broke at the very time Rebecca called with the news of a possible book deal. He was familiar enough with the book business to know that author advances were usually spaced out by payments in one-thirds: one-third paid on the signing of a contract; one-third on delivery and acceptance of a completed manuscript; and the last third on publication of the book. James was willing to agree to whatever was needed during the course of Rebecca's phone conversation, but she wouldn't listen.

James never liked being held to the rules. He especially didn't like being reminded of them when he was strapped for cash. James would go to lunch because he had no choice, but he resented everything about it. On his way to Orso, James speculated what the woman publisher's idea might be. Something derived from his travel pieces . . . probably a look back. Mindlessly predictable, but who cared? It was found money. He'd make his way though the obligatory lunch somehow, nodding in agreement with everything said. He'd sign a contract for whatever they wanted; and then he'd ignore whatever was expected of him and write what he wished to write.

Writing a novel wouldn't require travel . . . he'd just returned from an extensive trip and hadn't intended to take another so soon. It wouldn't bleed his advance with research expense. Best of all, it wouldn't interfere with afternoon assignations or evening plans. The more he thought about it, the more he liked the idea. He'd instruct Rebecca to insist on a sizable advance, one weighted with as much on-signing take as possible.

James Willoughby was considered differently by different categories of people. Most men thought of James as an entertaining derivation of their gender: successful with women but uninterested — and therefore unsuccessful — in making a living. Society women saw him as a rare commodity: an attractive heterosexual extra man for their dinner parties. His many sexual liaisons enjoyed him as a dalliance; they thought James too consumed with himself to be marriage material.

James considered himself underserved. He was genuinely confused by the way his life was going; it wasn't going as he had planned. Something was missing that should have been in place long ago . . . his due. And what exactly was his due? It was an unrestricted life enabled by financial independence. He was already in his late forties. The world had yet to make good on his due, but James was sure it would. In the meantime, James made practical use of his charm. Not in a manipulative way, not in a duplicitous way, but in a way that lacked contrition. He was a writer. He was an artist. If he couldn't afford whatever was needed, and others could, why shouldn't they pick up the tab?

At the time James arrived at Orso, he meant to indicate complete cooperation to John and the woman publisher. Intending to greet his benefactors as they arrived, James came early and stationed himself at the bar in the front. Now that he was at the bar, why not order a drink . . . a glass of red wine to take the edge off the crank; to round the sharp bends he'd need to maneuver when they showed up. James remembered it was a Thursday. Thursday was the day of the week that extremely aerobic waitress across the street went off duty after lunch.

James reflected further. He didn't really like Orso. It reminded him of a recent disappointment. He looked over at Table One. Table One was the spot where he and his play had been turned down by a theatrical producer. There was no reason he had to lunch at this particular restaurant. Not really. After all, the lunch was for him, on behalf of his talent.

Another glass of wine convinced James to find some degree of enjoyment to what, with every passing minute of his wait, he determined would be a boring ordeal. Enjoyment was far more likely located across the street, suggested the wine.

James saw John coming through the door. Throwing two twenty-dollar bills on the bar, he began walking toward him. Then he saw Isabel. She can't possibly be the publisher woman, he thought to himself. She must be — she's with John. Blithely announcing his intention to relocate the lunch as he brushed by his hosts, James strode across the street with the confidence of a man who had set the lead.

An hour and a half later, Isabel and John left James behind with the spectacle he'd made of himself. Returning to his apartment from the disaster of lunch, James sat on his couch, lit a cigar, poured an early-afternoon whisky, and took stock. He needed a book advance . . . there was no getting around it. There would be no getting around Isabel.

There was something else at stake besides the money. It turned out James was wrong about Isabel's book idea. She hadn't proposed a reminiscence of his travels. Isabel was interested in the less charted exploration of James's childhood. James was nimble skimming the surface. He wasn't as sure of himself in the deep waters. Isabel recognized the limitations James placed on his talent . . . she'd backed him right up against the wall of his habitual complacency. James hadn't expected that. In fact, everything about Isabel was what James hadn't expected. She rankled him. But within a remarkably short period of time, the idea of her managed to intrigue him. . . . Isabel Simpson became a beguilement stretching just beyond James's reach.

19

The next morning, Rebecca phoned Isabel, intending to apologize for James and to ask for a second meeting. Isabel was out of town until the following Monday.

Rebecca called John. He was in his room at the Knickerbocker Club, packing.

"James wants another meeting with Isabel," announced Rebecca.

"Surely you jest?"

"No."

"In God's name, why?"

"Because he thought about the book idea and realized it had merit."

"Becky, I don't buy any of it. He needs the money, doesn't he?"

"Probably. But that doesn't necessarily preclude an interest in her proposal."

"The only book that interests him is a checkbook," said John. "He wants a place in Isabel's budget *and* her bed. Knowing James, he probably thinks he'll get both."

"You're forgetting me in this, John. Regardless of her ludicrous age, I respect Isabel and intend to do business with her in the future. What makes you think I'd allow Willoughby to jeopardize that?"

John hadn't meant to insult Rebecca. "You're right, of course," he said.

"Regardless of whether there's a book in him, why do you think James would pursue Isabel after she did such a devastating job of humiliating him?" asked Rebecca.

John gave up trying to fold his clothes and hold the receiver at the same time.

"You know what comes to mind?" he asked while using his forward-leaning weight to push a wingback chair toward the window, which overlooked Central Park. "A letter I remember reading from Alice B. Toklas's published collection," he said as he sat down. "I can't recall who she wrote the letter to, but it's this hysterically funny description of Hemingway's first visit with Gertrude Stein."

"Okay . . . I'll take the bait, what happened?"

"According to Toklas, when they were first introduced, Hemingway realized something about Stein that set the course of their relationship."

"That she was a lesbian?" suggested Rebecca.

"For Christ's sake, Becky, Gertrude Stein looked like a linebacker in a dress, and she was living with another woman . . . of course he knew she was a lesbian. What he didn't expect — what he couldn't accept — was that she was obviously his intellectual equal."

"So . . . ?"

"So, what do you think was his reaction? Was it to revel in her intellect? Was it to share his with her? Not at all. It was to try to bed her, despite the fact she was singularly ugly and sexually unavailable."

"James is not Hemingway, and Isabel is far from a Gertrude Stein."

"Ah, but Rebecca, what never changes is the male instinct to display dominance."

"Oh *please!*" protested Rebecca. "You're sounding down-right agrarian."

"My point precisely," responded John. "Manhood is not an intellectual conceit. It comes from the base of the spine. How else would you explain men's stupid acts of heroism . . . and something as haplessly male as James Willoughby's request for a second meeting with the woman who's insulted him? I'm sure part of it is financially motivated. But, just maybe, right now he needs something more."

"And what might that be?" asked Rebecca.

"Pride," answered John. "She took it from him yesterday. She looked right at him and took it away in broad daylight. Today he wants it back."

"You're wrong," insisted Rebecca. "Anyone who really knows Willoughby knows he's a moral outlaw. He's shameless . . . and without shame there *is* no pride."

"He might be after something different this time," suggested John.

"Well, if it's respect, she'll make him work for it."

"All kidding aside, that could be James Willoughby's salvation," said John.

There was a break in their banter, but neither was ready to end the phone visit.

"Talk of Gertrude Stein makes me want to be in Paris," sighed Rebecca.

"What a good idea," said John. "Maybe it's the right time for a pilgrimage to Chartres. I've always wanted to see it. And while I'm having a spiritual reawakening surrounded with acres of stained glass, you can have a kind of retail version of one on the rue du Faubourg Saint-Honoré."

"God, John . . . that sounds divine. I feel the urge for a new Chanel suit, and the exchange rate is working in my favor right now. Why don't we go on the way to the Frankfurt Book Fair next month?"

"I'll phone from San Francisco in another few days," said John. "We'll make a plan."

20

As John was on a plane returning to San Francisco, Isabel was on another, landing in Chicago.

A phone call from her father had interrupted the budget meeting the previous day.

"I'm terribly sorry to disturb you in the office," was his ominous greeting.

"It's about Mother . . . ?" anticipated Isabel.

"I'm afraid so. Isabel, Miss Drake told me that at one time she'd given you Dr. Stutz's name and phone number. I assume he explained your mother's illness. . . ."

"Yes . . . I met with him . . . about two years ago."

"Well, your mother has had a bad run the last few months and needs to be hospitalized."

"Why is what you're telling me different from all the other times?"

"Because this time she hasn't cooperated."

"Just how uncooperative is she?"

"It's extremely unfortunate to have come to this —"

"To have come to what?"

"Your mother's always admitted herself voluntarily to hospitals . . . but now she has an unholy fear she'll die in one."

"Why would she believe that?

"Because her own mother did yesterday." Mr. Simpson cleared his throat. "You need to know I had no choice but to commit your mother this morning."

"Are you at the hospital?"

"No. I'm at O'Hare Airport on my way to London. If I stay here, it will only make matters worse. I've scheduled business in Europe for the next several weeks."

"Should I come to Chicago?"

"It's up to you. But if you do, Isabel, please understand your mother isn't the person you knew."

With no intent of sarcasm, Isabel asked, "And who would that be?"

The moment that followed was the only intersecting axis between Isabel and her father when the compelling question might finally have been asked: Why had he never told Isabel and her brother about their mother's history of mental illness? Isabel held on to the moment as long as she could, despite its code of silence. She held on to it, hoping her father would answer without being asked.

"I need to catch my plane. Safe journey . . . the weather here is ghastly," he said.

Isabel flew to Chicago the next day. An unread manuscript rested on her knees while she watched hard pellets of rain stream horizontally against the window. Isabel remembered her meeting with Dr. Stutz . . .

"Miss Simpson, do you know that your mother's mother is institutionalized?"

"I have a grandmother?"

"You do . . ."

"And a grandfather?"

"Not that I'm aware."

"How can you be aware of one, but not the other?"

"Because my inquiries were made at the sanatorium in Austria where your grandmother has been a patient."

"Is it the same illness as my mother's?"

"Yes."

"Where does she live when she's not hospitalized?"

"She was permanently committed forty years ago."

"The hospital must have kept records . . . it must have been her husband who committed her."

"No, it wasn't."

"Then who?"

"The courts."

"Why would a court of law have anything to do with committing my grandmother?"

"Because she tried to kill your mother, who was ten at the time."

One sentence two years ago — from someone she'd met a short time before it was spoken — shed light on the overshadowing enigma that was Isabel's mother. It also told of a grandmother Isabel never knew existed. Isabel diagrammed the sentence as Dr. Stutz spoke it. *She tried to kill your mother, who was ten at the time.* It consisted of twelve piercingly precise words; none contained more than two syllables.

Whatever comforts Isabel could find came from her heart. *Your mother loved you, but was afraid of being with you because of what her own mother had done to her.* Had her mind been given the opportunity, it would have insisted on an alternative explanation: Isabel's mother abandoned her as soon as she was born; Isabel's grandmother was murderously deranged; and insanity — like water seeking its own level — was flowing effortlessly from one generation to the next.

Another piece of information was required before Dr. Stutz could complete her mother's story.

"How? How did her mother try to kill her?" Isabel had asked.

"With a butcher knife," had been the grisly reply.

A prepositional clause isn't supposed to be able to stand on its own. This one could. This one drew strength from the still air surrounding it.

21

Isabel was barely able to make out the outline inside the hospital room.

"Hello, Mother," she said from the doorway.

There was no response. Isabel took a few steps into the room.

"Hello, Mother," she said again.

Mrs. Simpson was staring at the ceiling.

Isabel turned on the light and came closer. Nothing could have prepared her for what she saw.

Mental illness had reduced Tisza Simpson to something hardly human. She was pinned down in her hospital bed by four-point restraints. What must have been hours of crying had soaked both sides of the pillow. Isabel dried her mother's still-wet face with a corner of the bedsheet and covered the ankle restraints with the blanket bunched up around her mother's feet. Mrs. Simpson's hands had been tied — palms facing up — each to their respective bed rail.

Isabel noticed her mother's scars for the first time. Not the caterpillar-like scars on her wrists — the hatch-marked ones on the inside of her hands. Those scars had their own living history. Her mother's hand wounds, violently inflicted in childhood, had healed in a way that knotted her skin into the shapes of small starfish in the middle of her palms, foreshortening her tendons and making it difficult for her fingers to span the keyboard of a piano. Those scars were the reason she could never play the piano in the way she wanted . . . in the way she knew it was meant to sound.

Isabel walked over to the light switch, flipped it off, and sat in the dark. She imagined what her mother must have looked like as a ten-year-old girl. Isabel thought of the desperation the girl must have felt when she saw a knife bearing down too fast to escape . . . of the terror she must have known once she realized it was her own mother wielding the knife. Did the girl raise her hands instinctively to protect her face? Or was it as Isabel imagined . . . that the girl had reached out even though her mother was trying to harm her? Isabel imagined all of this . . . and then Isabel imagined stabbing that wouldn't stop . . . stabbing that slowed only slightly as it repeatedly punctured the soft flesh of small, outstretched palms.

Tisza Simpson was a quadratic equation of unremitting questions, but none of the answers would ever include Isabel. Since the very start of who she was, Isabel's stoicism refused to surrender to that heartfelt injury. She looked over at her mother, crucified to a hospital bed — a dark shadow in a darkened room — and realized she had exhausted her mental repertoire of tricks. No longer able to govern her feelings, with nothing left to save her from hurt, she wept.

Isabel wept for her mother's lost soul and for her own desolate self, possessed of so much but bereft of any real joy. Uncontrollable emotion racked her body. Her stomach emptied itself, and still Isabel retched dry heaves. The night nurse helped her out of the room. An orderly came in to mop the floor. Through it all, Tisza Simpson never stopped staring at the ceiling.

Isabel asked the nurse to page Dr. Stutz.

"What gives you the right to treat my mother this way?" Isabel demanded to know.

"She's a danger to herself."

"I don't believe that . . . she's catatonic, for God's sake."

"You don't have to. All that matters is that I do."

"You arrogant son of a bitch!" shouted Isabel. That she would raise her voice stunned her more than what she had said. In a less combative tone, she asked, "Why tie her to her bed?"

"Her mother died yesterday."

"I know that, my father told me. . . . So what?"

Before he could answer, Isabel did. "No . . . let me see if I get this on my own . . . it's so unbelievable, it must be true," she said snidely. "There was a grandmother I didn't know was alive until two years ago, when you told me she was in a lunatic asylum for trying to kill my mother. There's my mother, who's finally been committed . . . but only after a psychotic episode when she heard her mother had died. And let's not forget my father. He must be the rational one. . . . I can tell because he was the one who insisted for years that my mother's only problem was an inner ear infection."

Isabel lowered her voice to something barely audible. "One might have thought her mother's death would have put an end to it. But that would be too pat, wouldn't it, Doctor? The story will repeat itself . . . and it'll end the same way, won't it? She'll die here or some godforsaken place like here, won't she?"

"I'm afraid so," Dr. Stutz said without the slightest trace of pity.

Isabel's hand suddenly swung toward the doctor. He intercepted it in midair. "You should do something about your temper," he said before releasing his grip on her arm.

Isabel returned to New York that night. She phoned Ian. Then she phoned Monina.

"When you were a child, you saw something . . . didn't you?" asked Monina. "Something about your mother that haunts you."

Isabel remembered. By the time she heard the unholy sound in the Chintz Room, her mother had already cut herself . . .

First at the wrists, and then the neck. Isabel pushed open the door — flooding the darkened room with light. She stepped into blood. It had already defaced the peacock wallpaper and soaked the flowered uphol-stery. There seemed no end to it . . . spurting from punctures . . . gushing in a fast-flowing river from a deep gash . . . narrowing into tributaries that were congealing into glutinous rivulets.

Isabel's fear was brutally in control until her eye caught the glint of something shiny. Crewel scissors. Struggling to take them away, Isabel grabbed her mother's wrist, not realizing it had been crudely hacked to the bone. Isabel's little fingers dug into her mother's flayed flesh and held on for dear life. "Look what you've done! Look what you've done!" Isabel screamed over and over again.

A battalion of servants heard Isabel's screams. Vera swaddled Mrs. Simpson in linen sheets frantically stripped off the bed. After she saw her mother being driven away, Isabel went into the bathroom. Her saliva tasted bitter, like rust. She felt feverish. Then she felt the coolness of tile and porcelain.

"They found me wedged in a narrow space between the toilet and the bathtub."

"Where had you taken yourself?" asked Monina.

"To another place," Isabel replied.

2

Isabel was able to remember how she
loved James. . . . Its beginning had to do with
the color of the sky.

22

Isabel flipped through the phone messages accumulated during her day in Chicago.

"Good morning, Rebecca, I'm returning your call from Friday."

Rebecca began to apologize for James's lunch performance. Isabel interrupted, "Nothing said now could possibly excuse your Mr. Willoughby."

"I'm sure you're right . . . John told me that James provided an entirely new definition of poor taste."

"Well, I suppose I'm to blame as much as anyone. John warned me," said Isabel.

"Listen, Isabel, you'll think this perverse. . . . James wants a second meeting."

"Let me guess," Isabel said, "he has his eye on another pair of handmade shoes he can't afford."

"That might be. But he's also interested in your proposal; and I'm giving him the benefit of the doubt," said Rebecca.

Rebecca was an important agent. Isabel decided to be frank with what she would say to her, but careful in how she said it.

"I think his talent deserves the benefit of your doubt. I'm not sure he does."

"Why not?" asked Rebecca.

"No matter how good a writer, he doesn't appear to have any discipline," answered Isabel. "It's as though he's everywhere but nowhere at the same time. And even if I had confidence in his ability to finish a book, I'm not sure I want to work with him."

"Oh, dear . . . I hadn't realized it had been that bad," said Rebecca.

"It was fairly stunning. He revealed himself in a way difficult to ignore," said Isabel. "Rebecca, for one brief moment during the lunch, some part of me heard what I thought to be anti-Semitism. Could that possibly be?"

"Isabel! God, no! James isn't anti-Semitic . . . he's just insufferable — an unfortunate personality trait that avails itself of all denominations."

Isabel laughed. "I'm sure you're right . . . I'll tell you what, if he can pull together an outline and three good sample chapters, I'll consider another meeting. But not until then."

"That's fair enough," said Rebecca.

"And Rebecca —"

"Yes . . ."

"I want to make it very clear now that if I decide to take him on, there'll be a modest on-signing payment attached to the most immodest clause I can craft stipulating the return of every penny if he doesn't deliver on time."

"Okay."

"One more thing . . ."

"Yes?"

"I'll also be deducting the cost of a bottle of Dom Perignon."

That afternoon, John phoned Isabel from San Francisco. After they finished discussing business, he said, "Darling, you sound a little blue."

"Family . . ."

"I'm sorry," said John sympathetically.

"For what?"

"For whatever it's doing to you."

"'We've all been hurt in action' . . . or so says I'm not sure who."

"Charles Dickens."

"What about Charles Dickens?" asked Isabel.

"He said that."

"Really?"

"Really. His mother had a misguided sense of priorities and forced him into child labor so she could pay her dressmaker."

"Jesus, how do any of us survive our parents?"

"We don't, darling . . . not one of us manages to get away clean. Dickens's childhood was so awful, you couldn't possibly have invented it. The good news for the rest of us is that it gave him great material."

"Well, I suppose that's one way of thinking of it . . ." Isabel trailed off.

"I have an idea," suggested John. "Why don't you join Rebecca and me in Paris before the Frankfurt Book Fair? You could sit in a Left Bank café and watch life go by while I find a greater meaning to it at Chartres and Becky does the same at Chanel."

Isabel was delighted by the invitation.

"Well? What say you?" asked John.

"Who's taking care of hotel reservations?"

"Leave everything to me."

Rebecca had yet to speak to James about his book. She agreed with Isabel: James was best when he wrote short. Rebecca wasn't the kind of agent who'd encourage a next step knowing her client couldn't fulfill his obligations. When she heard from

John that Isabel would be joining them in Paris, Rebecca realized something had to be done about James. She phoned him.

"James, I've managed a second chance with Isabel Simpson."

"I knew you would . . . you're the consummate diplomat," he said.

His delight made Rebecca snap.

"I've just about had it, so listen carefully," she said. "If you're interested in writing the book, you'll need to hand in a proposal and three good chapters. By 'a proposal,' I mean something that runs at least ten pages and describes the beginning, middle, and end of your story. And by 'three sample chapters,' I mean three sample chapters of at least ten pages each. Not five-page chapters; not two chapters instead of three. . . . Do I make myself clear?"

"You certainly do. Rebecca, my dear, you sound downright paramilitary."

Rebecca ignored James's attempt to trivialize their exchange. "Assuming Isabel agrees to a contract, don't expect a large on-signing payment."

"Why not?"

"Because she's scoped you out."

"What an extremely unpleasant thing to say. I suppose that's the kind of expression used in an office."

"James, you've underestimated her once. You'd be an even bigger jerk the second time."

"I don't know what you're talking about, so I'll just ignore that last gratuitously vitriolic comment. But since you're issuing orders like Captain Vere, tell me when I should get this to you."

"Within the next few weeks. I'll be in Paris with John and Isabel on our way to Frankfurt in early October. If she likes what you've written, I'll come to terms with her before we leave."

"You're several steps ahead of me . . . precisely where one's agent should be," said James.

Rebecca was in no mood. "Just do your bit, and don't screw up."

23

Shortly after Rebecca and James's phone conversation, his father died. Unexpectedly.

When James asked his mother how, she informed him in unforgiving terms, "The doctor says it was a massive heart attack, but I think your father had outlived his purpose."

During the years George Willoughby was outliving whatever his wife thought to be a purpose, his debt compounded itself many times over. It presented itself to Mrs. Willoughby the day after her husband was interred.

With the exception of an ancestral portrait — and several less important dog paintings — the previous generation of Willoughbys had off-loaded everything of any discernable value left by the generation before. The ponderously heavy eighteenth-century furniture; the nineteenth-century Herter Brothers sideboard with inlaid tiles of Aesop's fables; the blue Chinese export porcelain . . . all sold. As a boy, one of James's few delights in the estate's bleakly stripped-down interior were the dog paintings that hung in the upstairs hall. He especially liked the one whose name, Admiral, had been awarded its own copper plaque on the painting's frame.

James came home from school one afternoon, and in exact

dimensions where the paintings had been, there were unfaded squares of originally colored silk wallpaper. James knew enough not to ask questions. He assumed the paintings had gone the way of everything else in his home . . . to auction. When Mr. Willoughby alluded to the subject that evening, Mrs. Willoughby's only comment conveyed such sharp disdain, its words sliced through the dining room's musty air.

"Only poseurs would want paintings of another family's dogs hanging on their walls," she said.

Death, debt, and divorce are crucial suppliers on which the auction houses depend for inventory. After George Willoughby's death, there was no choice but to cash in the last salable asset that wasn't Willoughby land — a small Sargent portrait of James's great-great-grandfather. The Willoughbys couldn't afford to wait for the next scheduled sale at Sotheby's. James made arrangements to sell the painting directly to the Tate. After its proceeds paid down a legacy of bills, the remaining cash went to Mrs. Willoughby, who wrote a generous check to her son.

James returned to New York flush and newly leisured. He decided to attend a wedding in London, preceded by a weekend in Paris, where he had been invited to an opera at Versailles. James phoned Rebecca's office to ask when she'd be arriving in Paris. Upon hearing her dates and his overlapped, James asked for the name of her hotel. He assumed Isabel would be staying there as well.

Richard Cobb, an Englishman, once observed, "Wonderful country France . . . Pity about the French!" Isabel believed Paris, regardless of how disagreeable its citizens, was the world's most captivating place to be; and that the French, despite their inhospitality, reminded the less-civilized rest of us that a good life was where you found its pleasures.

Isabel, Rebecca, and John were staying at a small hotel on the Left Bank. The Hôtel Duc de Saint-Simon is discreetly perched on the rim of one of Paris's most charming streets, the rue du Bac. Rebecca took a room on the hotel's top floor, facing the street. John and Isabel had rooms next to each other, facing the back garden. Rebecca had a dinner date with a French publisher. Isabel and John were on their own that night.

Shortly after he'd settled into his room, John's phone rang. It was James.

"Hello . . . John? I'm in Paris, and I wanted to take you and Miss Simpson out for dinner tonight."

There was stunned silence instead of a response.

"In order to reciprocate for your New York lunch," explained James.

"How on earth did you know we were in town, much less at this hotel?" asked John incredulously.

"I read the news of your arrival in the *International Herald Tribune* on my flight over," James said with laconic wit.

Realizing it was unlikely he'd receive any meaningful disclosure, John asked a practical question.

"Where are you staying?"

"With friends on avenue Foch."

"Why am I not surprised . . ."

"I've made reservations for all of us at À Sousceyrac," said James.

"How very confident of you, but I seriously doubt you'll convince Isabel to partake in the culinary experience."

"Why not?"

"I'll tell you why not . . . because even if you were in town to personally fund an orphanage for Algerian children, you'd never be able to make up for the vile first impression you provided in New York."

There was a self-conscious pause before James volunteered, "Maybe not . . . but at least allow me the attempt."

The unexpected appearance of humility softened John.

"Well, as it happens, this is the one night we had no real plans. It would need to be an early dinner, because I've hired a car to drive me to Chartres first thing tomorrow morning."

"Whatever is best . . . ," said James hopefully.

"Hold on. . . . I'll knock on her door and ask."

If confusion had pure expression, it was Isabel's face.

"You can't possibly be serious!"

"He's the one with the sought-after dinner reservation, and he's as serious as I've ever heard him."

"How did he even know we were here?"

"I've no idea, but he's holding on the line for our answer."

"Where's his handler?" asked Isabel, sounding panicked. "Where is Rebecca?"

"Rebecca won't be any help. She's left already."

"Well, get her back!"

"Isabel, don't be ridiculous. She's in the middle of dinner with Eugene Bromunk. At this very moment, she's probably trying to convince him to part with his francs."

"What should we do? I have absolutely no intention of breaking bread with that man, no matter how well reviewed the restaurant. Is he alone?"

"He's somebody's houseguest, and from the address, it sounds posh. They're included in tonight's dinner."

"That's probably because they're paying for it."

"I'm sure . . . but think of it this way: their layers of three-ply cashmere might buffer us from James's boorish behavior. I told him an early evening. We can always make excuses if he becomes impossible." Then John added, "We're in Paris, Isabel, nothing can go too wrong."

Somehow, often against impossible odds, John was always able to put things right. Isabel's stricken face relaxed into a smile.

"So is that a yes?" asked John.

24

Scientific research has proven that long-term memories reside permanently in a section of the brain called the hippocampus; and short-term memory is temporarily stored in a different section located in the precortal cortex. Quantitative science can explain short-term memory loss. What has yet to be explained is why one is able to retrieve certain long-term memories, but not others.

Even though Isabel wasn't able to remember why she tried to kill her husband, she was completely sure of when it was — the very instant it was — that her love for him began. Odd as it sounds, in part it had to do with the color of the sky.

There's something to be said about the autumn sky in Paris and how its light magically interacts with the city's architecture. During certain times of the day — especially at blue-gray dusk — the narrow streets often seem as though they're stage sets wherein everything is lighted in the most illogical and beautiful way.

James stepped out of the car that had pulled up to the entrance of Saint-Simon just at the point when the early-evening sky was turning its own different color. As Isabel was coming down the hotel's shallow bank of stairs to street level, and James was coming around the car to open its door on her side, he appeared illuminated from behind by the day's last rays.

Unlike their previous and only other meeting, they had a good look at each other. The French call it "the seeing eye." In the brief time it took Isabel to descend four stairs, she saw in James something she hadn't expected . . . something below his surface. And as he came around the car to open Isabel's door, James saw something in Isabel that offered him an entirely different kind of optimism: he saw what he thought was a most lovely face . . . and on it, he recognized a subtle expression of surprised delight.

That was the instant, thought Isabel years later. That instant was the beginning of them.

À Sousceyrac is a small restaurant in a bohemian section of the eleventh arrondissement. Michelin's recently awarded third star resulted in an impossibly long waiting list for reservations. James had managed a table.

Several bottles of wine were ordered, and the waiter suggested a first course of *belon*. A polite exchange was had among the five of them in both French and English before the langoustines arrived and James could turn his attention exclusively to Isabel.

It's impossible to piece together why two people have a reciprocal attraction. If you single out each individual reason and consider it alone, it often seems unreasonable. Timing has a great deal to do with it — a factor least likely admitted because it requires acknowledging romance to be dependent on luck, and not the other way around. It happened that when they met in Paris, both Isabel and James — each with their own emotional dichotomy — wanted to belong to someone other than themselves.

At the time, Isabel had begun to wonder whether the world would ever allow her life some gaiety. James Willoughby's New York debut had been a disaster, but in Paris he presented himself in a more favorable light. In Paris, Isabel thought James had unique charm. She liked his bravado, and the jaunty way he looked — just this side of foppishness. She liked the way he thought — he possessed a nuanced sensibility and was well read. She especially liked the idea of liking him in the mangled moments he was so difficult to like. The implicit danger of James made him sexually alluring.

It would be a professional conflict of interest if Isabel were to accept James's personal attentions when he also expected her to publish his book. That issue will need to be cleared up, she concluded as the dinner was winding down.

At the same time Isabel was hoping for some well-deserved gaiety in her life, James had begun to wonder whether the world would ever provide him a sense of stability. He was getting too old to be sleeping with so many women. He was tired of the haphazardness with which his days took shape, and he was not unaware of the increased amount he'd been drinking. He liked the way Isabel looked — she was soignée, she had grace. He liked the way she thought, with strength and decisiveness — she reminded him of being able to see all the way down to the bottom of a deep pond. But she was also a complicated creature . . . more than he was used to handling in a woman, which offered the possibility of danger. James found that sexually alluring.

As dessert was served, James thought to himself, She probably won't be available if she thinks I expect her to publish my book. He hadn't really wanted to write a novel. Now that he had some money, there was no more reason to. James would make sure Isabel knew he'd changed his mind about the book; then he would invite her to the opera at Versailles. Once James made that decision, he made another . . . one that surprised even him. He decided it was important for Isabel to see him pay for dinner that night.

25

As he bid good night to Isabel and John, James let it be known that he no longer intended to write a book. When he phoned the next morning, Isabel felt free to accept his invitation to that evening's event at Versailles.

Versailles, in a low valley between two lines of wooded hills, was the lucky location for Louis XIII's hunting lodge, which he had subsequently upgraded into a chateau. Louis XIV, determined to build a lasting monument to his own reign, remolded the chateau to an over-the-top level of grandeur. In 1684, the daily workforce required 22,000 men and 6,000 horses; its exorbitant expense impoverished the county. Before discontent among his citizens festered into rebellion and rebellion triggered the Revolution — leaving Versailles an empty shell — life at court, with all of its rituals and intrigues, was vividly described in the memories of the duc de Saint-Simon . . . a coincidence James pointed out when he and Isabel arrived at the front gate.

In its original incarnation, the chateau was entered by twenty-two different gates. Only those lucky few who possessed the right to bring their coach into the great courtyard of the Louvre were granted the right to enter the chateau by way of its main entrance.

The same tier system was employed three hundred years later. Patrons who gave $150,000 or more toward the foundation hosting the gala that evening were welcomed at the main gate, while others were shunted to side entrances. Placed on a complimentary list by an anonymous board member, James and "guest" were invited through the front door. The opera, performed in the Salle de Spectacles, was *Diana and Acteon*.

A dinner jacket made James his most confident. He was aware of being noticed when he entered the reception room, and especially pleased to be seen escorting Isabel. Wearing a simple slip dress cut on the bias, Isabel was the least-adorned woman at the grand event. Despite or because of that, she also was noticed.

After the opera, patrons were shown to dinner in the Galerie des Glaces. Sponsors, on the other hand, were flushed directly from the opera hall into the courtyard, cold-shouldered and unfed. James and Isabel remained with the patrons and were seated across a table too large to allow them to converse with each other.

James settled on familiar ground — sandwiched between two socialites — but his focus was on Isabel, a pastiche of cadmium red lipstick, milk white skin, and eyes the color of peridot. Her mass of wavy, black hair was piled on top of her head. She also had the surrounding men leaning into what she was saying. James strained to pick up verbal fragments that might identify the topic of their animated exchange. The little he heard didn't make sense. What the hell is "cost of goods sold"? he wondered. It took him a while to realize they were discussing the global price fluctuations of paper.

The last thing that would normally interest James was a conversation about commodities, but he very much wanted to be on the other side of the table with Isabel. James was all too familiar with the politesse of dinner parties: he was obliged to entertain the two women flanking him. Any other night he'd be able to do it without thinking. It involved a repartee that would show them off, but not tax their conversational range. He knew to divide himself equally — staggering the time spent — between both women, starting with the woman on his right.

The woman to James's right was everything he'd known sitting to his right for the past twenty years. Suzie Evans was a rich American whose father had made a fortune in the poultry business. James was sure that if there were a husband in the vicinity, his empty look would identify him. "Shadow men" is what James called men who traded their souls in a Faustian bargain for their wives' money. James mentally counted the number of times he had sought out the possibilities of rich women. There but for the grace of God go I, he said to himself after recognizing Mr. Evans by his vacant expression.

Mrs. Evans wore an ensemble women of a certain age and wealth all seem to have agreed upon: a taffy-colored evening gown and a globular strand of South Sea pearls. She was the anonymous board member who had arranged James's arrival through the front door. She was also the gala's most generous patron, and had requested James be seated to her left. Not surprisingly, she got what she wanted . . . but the debonair object of her want seemed to be spending too much time trained on the unaccessorized woman across from them.

"Who is that woman? . . . I don't understand her hair," Mrs. Evans said earnestly to James, not knowing of his connection to Isabel.

"I dare say you never will," James quipped.

Reckless, reckless James had just bitten the social hand that fed him. But he didn't care. He reveled in the idea that Isabel's hair — and everything else about her — was a mystery to a very different member of the same sex seated next to him.

To make up for his restaurant switch in New York, James offered a nightcap anywhere Isabel wished. She suggested the Lancaster Hotel on the rue de Berri.

"So, why this particular spot?" asked James when they arrived.

"It feels like London in Paris. And since you'll soon be leaving one for the other, I thought it might help you acclimatize. Besides, it has something in its bar you're bound to appreciate tonight."

Even from the entrance, James spotted the something. It stood on a pedestal in front of the bar's large painting by Boris Pastoukhoff, a 1930s portrait artist who had often paid his hotel bills with still lifes.

James slipped his arm around Isabel's waist. "You're my glamorous inside joke," he said as they walked to a small table near the marble statue of Diana.

Isabel was a remote woman best admired at a distance. Even at close range, very few people saw beneath her frosty surface.

James did.

Over drinks under the statue of Diana at the Lancaster Hotel, James was keenly aware of the least obvious part of Isabel . . . her idiosyncratic take on life. That night, James finally realized what he wanted. It wasn't what he planned. It had nothing to do with the gradations of background or the allure of money. It had to do with Isabel.

John stayed up waiting for Isabel to return. When he heard the hotel's heavy keys jingle in the hallway next door, he ordered room service for both of them.

Muffled in the hotel's terry-cloth robes, they sat on John's bed, drinking tea, eating madeleines, and debriefing one another on their respective evenings.

"Before the most delicious dinner of rabbit stew with Rebecca, I went to an AA meeting at Saint-Sulpice," said John. "God, I was grateful to be an imported drunk, because I can't imagine being an alcoholic trying to stay sober in a country that produces over two hundred and fifty different kinds of red wine." And then, without pausing, he asked, "So how do you feel about your future husband leaving for London tomorrow morning?"

Isabel was undone.

"What a remarkable thing to say. Why would you say it?"

"Because I studied you both the other night. It occurred to me that you and James are like weirdly exotic creatures in a rain forest. Before stumbling upon each other, neither of you could have imagined there was more than one of your kind."

"Stop it." Isabel laughed. Realizing she was blushing, she blushed more. "It's not possible."

"Why not?" asked John.

"Because."

"Because?"

"'He's impossible' . . . it was the first thing that came out of your mouth when I suggested we contact him. You were right . . . he's hopelessly impossible. And that makes us impossible."

"He is," said John. "He absolutely is . . . but the only thing that really matters is, he's trying not to be. In fact, he's trying to be possible for you. He paid for dinner last night. That has to be a first for him."

"James Willoughby is the kind of man who dooms a love affair from the start," insisted Isabel. "I'd have to be a fool to think it would last . . . so I'd be an even greater fool to allow it a beginning."

"Isabel, darling, it's already begun. Listen to a dying man. Take a fool's chance." John looked at Isabel with the calmness of a man who had come to terms.

"No, John . . . you're wrong!" Isabel insisted angrily, as if she could command his health back into place. She had sensed something for weeks. Now that John finally told her, she refused to accept it.

"One word says I'm right. Lymphoma."

Isabel couldn't control her sobbing. She didn't try.

"Don't, dear girl," John reassured. "I promise we'll both be fine. . . . I've had an awfully good run. And it's not entirely over . . . there's still my exit. Until then, I'm determined to enjoy myself. Tomorrow morning we'll go across the street and I'll buy the most beautiful teal-colored bow tie. I saw it in a window after the store closed."

The next morning, before they left for Frankfurt, Isabel bought John the tie. Like a bookmark left in its place even though the reader continued ahead, it would always be a reminder of where — in Isabel's story — one part ended and the other began.

26

Isabel accepted James's invitation to dinner shortly after she returned to New York. He opened his apartment door . . . they never made it to the bed.

Wearing an antique silk kimono she found in James's closet, Isabel leaned against the kitchen counter and watched him prepare their dinner.

"Five tricks to cooking risotto: One, imported arborio rice. Two, homemade broth — this is a reduction of the pheasant I boiled last week and froze. Three, stir with a wooden spoon — don't stop stirring once you've begun. Four, remove from the flame prematurely — it continues to cook from its own heat. Five, serve from the skillet — it congeals into a less creamy consistency if it's transferred onto a serving platter."

As James was listing his five steps of ensuring delicious risotto, Isabel was reconciling her own numbered parts. Mind, sex, and — most remarkable — her heart were working as one and had miraculously found their correspondents in the same man.

Over his protests, Isabel returned to her own bed that night. As she eased into a bath, soapy water stung raw marks on the more angular parts of her that had come into contact with the vestibule's sisal carpet beneath them. The evidentiary remains of their lovemaking was her ripped dress, lying disheveled on the bathroom floor,

Outside Isabel's office hours, they were inseparable that week. Wherever they went, the women greeting James with over-familiarity warned Isabel of what had so indiscriminately preceded her. But it made no matter. James had taken up residency in Isabel's present. The past was the past and belonged to the previous women. Nothing before Isabel made a difference to her — not even the fact that James's before-the-now included a suspiciously short-term marriage. It was to an Italian . . . that's how he knew so much about risotto.

Had Isabel been more worldly, she would have understood that the past is not necessarily just the past. She would have understood that the past is attached to the present; and that the present informs the future. James's past affairs were legion. One with a particularly bad outcome instilled an irrational conviction at age thirty-three that it was time for him to take a wife. James made that life-changing decision on a Thursday. Friday, he met an unattached *principessa* at her mother's dinner party. They went to the Italian consulate for the necessary papers on Monday morning and were married at city hall that afternoon. By Tuesday, James realized he might have acted too rashly.

Like the next verse to the same song, James repeated his father's mistake of relying on marriage to make up for what he believed to be his life's shortfall. Having banked on his bride's family, James discovered after the fact that they were cash-poor. They had an aristocratic provenance, a villa in the foothills of Lucca, but no money. Not only was there no money, his bride was a manic-depressive, which explained — also after the fact — her willingness to be rushed to the altar.

James started to suspect something was amiss when she asked

him to accompany her to the dentist's office the day after they were married. The reason she'd been staying with her mother in New York had to do with a necessary root canal not entrusted to her dentist in Rome. She'd already recovered from the procedure by the time James met her. Why would she want me there for a final checkup? he wondered. James had known his wife for only a few days, and so he knew her not at all. Perhaps she was anxious, he thought; perhaps she wanted him to hold her hand.

His wife needed support of a less sentimental kind. Instead of James holding her hand, she held his . . . and led him to the front desk where, to his astonishment, she expected him to settle her outstanding account. James reluctantly drew out his checkbook, asked the receptionist for a pen, and thought, Nothing could be more annoying. But there could be — and there was. He was presented with a five-figure bill as his brand-new bride told him she had no dental insurance.

His wife's expensive teeth were just the start to an alarming series of revelations. A week after James arrived at what he assumed would be their own residence — an enormous seventeenth-century villa that included an Orsetti garden — he was greeted by the other tenants . . . her relatives, back from holiday. The only member of the family not living with them was her mother. She'd met a New York architect during his year at the American Academy in Rome and ran off with him long ago.

James's precarious position as spouse was pushed over the brink by a single piece of paper: a food bill handed to him by his sister-in-law at the end of his first married month.

"You have taken my sister as your own," she explained in impeccable English. "That includes the cost of her food at the villa. I have . . . how do you Americans say? I have *prorated* the bill. It is only fair, after all."

James vigorously argued that his wife had eaten on the house all her life. His rebuttal held no ground; he fled to New York and filed for divorce.

Because his wife refused to hire an attorney, James found himself in the financially overextended position of paying for both sets of lawyers. An affair with his own defrayed some of the expenses . . . until he left her, and she retroactively charged him her full billable hours.

In the fifteen years since, James had stepped away from several chances to remarry. Now there was Isabel, a woman who expected to be loved seriously. James intended to become her husband.

A man provides a woman all of the crucial information about himself within the first few hours they meet. Within the first hour of being introduced, James had made known to Isabel through how he behaved and expressed himself that he wasn't interested in making money but very interested in having it; that he was conventionally well mannered but erratically principled; and that he was gifted but undisciplined.

Even before she made love with James, Isabel prevented herself from addressing fundamental, obvious issues. Her heart wanted what it wanted. Isabel perceived James to be a man who was financially unmotivated because he never had cause to be otherwise. With Isabel in his life, he would have cause. She heard a man who was feckless when he drank. With her by his side, there would be fewer reasons to drink. Once they made love — and it was fatally clear to both of them they were meant to be together — Isabel was sure James would change. He would change on the pretext of love . . .

. . . And so it went with Isabel's undisciplined heart. That was how she convinced her mind, which was busy being seduced by James's intellect, that nothing else mattered.

There is a French expression, *coup de foudre:* love at first sight. If you translate the words literally, they mean something different . . . something dangerous: "a blow of lightning." Less than a week after their risotto dinner, James asked Isabel for marriage. Had she known that his proposal to the first Mrs. James Willoughby was equally impetuous, it would have made absolutely no difference. Isabel's answer still would have been yes . . . a heedless, headlong yes.

27

"What splendid news! When?" asked John.

"I thought in six months. Sometime in June. Is that all right by you?" asked Isabel.

"I can last until then."

"Of course you will," said Isabel. "And if you begin to fade, you'll tell me, and I'll move it up. Will you promise to tell me?"

"Don't worry. I won't bow out before making sure you're properly launched. Where will the big event take place?"

"It's his second marriage, so I don't think a church wedding," said Isabel.

"Big mistake," insisted John. "There's more ceremonial gravitas to a church wedding. People behave better in a church. They even look better . . . the pews make them sit up straighter."

"I can't see myself being walked down an aisle; and James would prefer a civil ceremony at his family's place in Virginia."

"I think that's terribly generous of you, darling, but have you been there yet?"

"No . . . why?"

"It's like a Ralph Lauren ad on acid."

"That bad?"

"I kid you not."

"We're going there this weekend, and then on to Chicago to meet my father."

"Brace yourself for both," suggested John. "My other line is ringing. . . . I'll check in tomorrow."

It was Rebecca calling. James had just told her of his engagement to Isabel.

"John, did you hear the unbelievable news?"

"I have."

"Well, what are you doing about it? You're the only one she'll listen to. For God's sake, do something before she becomes fodder for the columns," demanded Rebecca. "By then there'll be no controlling it."

"I'm not at all sure what you think 'it' is; but what makes you think anything should be done?"

"Are you mad?" Before John could defend his state of mind, she answered for him. "It would be a complete disaster!"

"Why?"

"You *are* mad! Because James Willoughby isn't meant to be more than a three-day affair."

"Your arithmetic is already wrong. It's been more than three days . . . it's been five."

"Three days, five days . . . what difference does it make? She can't possibly believe he wants what she wants."

"I think they both want what any of us wants . . . to be happy. And they seem to be that with each other."

Rebecca ignored John's sentiment. "What's happened to the girl? She's always been so clear-sighted. It has to be the sex. It's pulled her out to sea like a deadly undertow."

"Why not wish them well? . . . He's your client."

"John, we both know this man. This is a man who has a history with women and their bank accounts . . . Isabel should be told." Instead of giving John an opportunity to respond, Rebecca continued coercing. "If you don't do something, someone should. There's a brother somewhere in the pampas. He's a cattleman. That requires an unarguable kind of masculinity. He probably carries a gun."

"Becky . . . *really!*"

"Well, at least that would put an end to it. In that part of the world, eliminating an inappropriate suitor before he marries your sister must be as common as shooting a rabid dog. Why are you driveling platitudes when you should be talking sense to her?"

A momentary lapse in Rebecca's rant gave John a chance to weigh in. "You've all but laid out my argument," he said.

"I don't see how . . ."

"Think about it for a moment. Everyone assumed James would marry money. But he's ceded to something entirely different. You're absolutely right: James has a history with women and their trust funds. The point you're missing is that he's chosen a woman who doesn't have one. Isabel earns a living, and she'll expect the same of James. Marriage to Isabel will make James better than he deserves to be. He knows that. It won't be easy. He knows that too. He must be very much in love . . . don't you think?"

Rebecca didn't answer.

"As for Isabel, she's finally met her match," John said with delight. "Without James, she would have become brittle with control. With him, she'll learn to bend. He'll bring spontaneity and an entirely different perspective. I find whatever you're calling 'it' deeply romantic."

Rebecca still didn't answer.

"Come on, Becky, wish them well. If nothing else, they show each other off beautifully. They remind me of stylish bookends."

That brought a laugh from Rebecca. "Well, I'm afraid I'm too cynical to be persuaded that a man changes for the love of a good woman," she said. "But I suppose there's something to be said for the fact they look great together. People have married for less."

28

Dinner conversation with Mrs. Willoughby was more naming of names than conversation.

There was talk of certain people, certain schools, and certain marriages. Everyone and everything Mrs. Willoughby mentioned seemed to be interconnected. People's behavior fell into two categories: "attractive" and "unattractive." Advantages or injustices befalling them were measured in terms of inheritance.

While passing the hollandaise sauce, Mrs. Willoughby told of a good friend whose valuable ruby necklace was unfairly left to a second cousin, rather than the sister. Isabel was at a loss to understand why such a flimsy issue deserved the weight of its discussion, but she listened patiently as Mrs. Willoughby continued.

"At least it stayed in the family. The Keswicks lost all of the family jewelry to the attending nurse. You have to pay particular attention to the staff in retirement communities. They take unbridled advantage of the more addled residents."

"Really," was the best Isabel could think of saying.

"And what of your family, Isabel?" asked Mrs. Willoughby.

"Well, there are my parents and a brother . . ."

"Surely you have more family than that?"

"No," said Isabel without going further.

When Mrs. Willoughby pressed her for details, Isabel remained as nondescript as possible. She didn't know how to explain the strangeness of what Mrs. Willoughby would have referred to as "Simpson background."

What Isabel learned of the Willoughby family tugged in the opposite direction to her own. Generations of Willoughbys managed to do nothing in the exact same place. Simpson ancestors steadfastly refused to settle in one location for fear they'd be missing whatever adventure might be in another. The Willoughby dynasty was like a large, sedate organism. Generations of the dispersed Simpson family had lived off the grid. They were renegades behaving at best questionably, and for the most part very badly indeed. Isabel's "background" consisted of lawlessness on one side and insanity on the other, with murderous exploits marring both.

Isabel wasn't defensive about her background. It just seemed that if she were to describe her family, Mrs. Willoughby might be uneasy with the specifics of a wealthy father who didn't believe his money became his children's by default; a mother who was institutionalized; and an overeducated brother who was living in the bush. Still, Isabel hoped she made a good impression. She very much wanted to be liked by Mrs. Willoughby. She knew how important it was to James.

Rufus Simpson received his daughter and future son-in-law with the excuse that his wife was "indisposed." After their short visit, he went through considerable trouble to reach Ian, who was not easily located.

"Willoughby personifies a certain type of New England private school cleverness," Mr. Simpson said to his son over the phone. His tone was harsh. "And he spent far too much time admiring my paintings."

"What about Isabel? Does she look happy?" asked Ian.

"Very. . . . She's clearly in love."

"Well, don't you think that's the most important thing?"

"Yes, of course . . . but there's something about him that makes me worry for her."

"It's like our very own *Canterbury Tales*. So where else do we need to go, and who else must we see about our marriage?" asked James.

The third and last leg of their premarital pilgrimage was to Monina.

"Why don't I meet him at his apartment?" suggested Monina, who knew she'd glean more about the man if she saw James in his own setting.

"Well?" asked Isabel the next morning.

"He'll be interesting company for you."

The silence between them became tactile.

"And?" asked Isabel.

"And he drinks. . . . So do I. The difference is that I live alone. I don't know how drink plays out with another person under the same roof, especially with one who doesn't."

"He'll slow down when we're married. . . . What else?"

"His shoes."

"What about them?"

"The shoes aren't what concern me. It's what the shoes imply. Have you considered the implications of his handmade shoes?"

"He's a man of taste," said Isabel, sounding pleased.

"As long as you understand he's expensive . . ."

29

The first time Isabel made an excuse for James was in winter.

A colleague of Isabel's had a weekend house in the same town as hers. Isabel and James had been invited to a Friday dinner. There had been too much drink. It required an apology Saturday morning.

Isabel remembered how she managed it — how she apologized for something she refused to acknowledge. She did it by deceiving herself with artfully designed words.

"Dinner was great fun. . . . I'm sure you'll forgive James's rambunctious behavior," was the facile way she put it.

Isabel insisted they go cross-country skiing that weekend.

"Bloody hell . . . I need a valet," swore James while he struggled to snap his boot onto its ski. "She'll have me climbing K-2 next . . . and once we've covered snowbound terrain, she'll move us into deep jungles to search for El Dorado."

"That's actually not a bad idea," said Isabel. "I should put your manhood to the test before we marry."

"I agree completely. In fact, why don't we skip the outdoors this morning and return to bed. I have the most voluptuous idea of just how to provide proof."

"I don't mean manhood in that way. I mean your male

courage. I think I should put that to the test . . . preferably in an obscure location on the brink of war."

"You've read too much Joseph Conrad, my dear," said James.

"All right . . . no war. But I insist on a foreign land. One with a turbulent history."

Isabel thought further while James continued to struggle with his skis.

"I have it!" she exclaimed.

"Well, I don't," groused James. "These skis are a damn nuisance."

"We'll go to South America — and, assuming you survive the test, we'll visit my brother afterward."

"Rio de Janeiro is as far afield as I'll travel," said James. "I could finally replenish my dwindling supply of guarana."

"I know the perfect location. It has all the dominant themes: life-threatening diseases, fearsome creatures, hostile tribes."

"Where might this be?" asked James, beginning to sense Isabel was losing sight of the joke.

"The Amazon."

When Isabel booked the plane tickets the following week, James learned his future wife had the disconcerting habit of doing what she said.

From the air, the Amazon looks like a vast green carpet; its river like a sinuous, shimmering ribbon. Isabel charted their excursion. They began at Iquitos, and would journey — by way of cargo boat — downriver, arriving four days later in Leticia. Isabel was the only woman aboard the small boat. James and Isabel were the only foreigners, and the only passengers not transporting produce.

James's joke about El Dorado wasn't too far off the mark. When they were youngsters, Isabel and her brother entertained each other by recounting the myths of lost civilizations. As the riverboat drifted downstream the first day of their adventure, Isabel told James about the great stone cities described in *The Chronicles of Akakor.*

"The *Chronicles* were written by 'those chosen by the gods,'" Isabel set her story.

James — smoking a Cuban cigar — swung back and forth in a hammock on deck. "Did the gods descend from a mountain?" he asked.

"Not this time," said Isabel. "These particular gods were described as 'white-skinned strangers' who arrived by way of golden airships."

"The idea of golden airships is a bit far-fetched," said James.

"I suppose you're right," agreed Isabel. "That part of the myth sounds like a Las Vegas floor show. The point you need to concentrate on is that they civilized the tribe that built stone cities stretching from Bolivia to Venezuela, linked by the most intricate system of underground tunnels. No one can explain it."

"It seems to me the dynamic white-skinned strangers were on a suspiciously westernized mission," James joked. "First they forced industrialization, and then they mobilized commerce. Was Akakor the CEO?"

"Akakor was one of the larger cities. And before you make too much fun, there was a recent discovery of pyramids by satellite images . . . and they correlate with the location description in the *Chronicles.*"

"Well, like any good myth, I'm sure the lost cities are protected by a curse of death, so I think we should just leave it be, satellite images or no. We're docking shortly. I, for one, have no intention of inquiring among the natives," said James. "It will just stir them up."

"The humid air has made me lazy. . . . I'll take your place in the hammock," Isabel said. "Be sure and wear your boots. I've read that there're twenty-six different kinds of poisonous snakes. The ones not hanging from trees hide in the undergrowth near the water."

"No doubt they all pool information about the boat schedules," replied James. He leaned over to kiss Isabel, who smiled at him drowsily.

Isabel fell asleep to the pleasant smell of the shoreline's warm grass. She roused herself when she thought she heard James return to the boat, and then drifted back to sleep. James woke her before dinner.

"Darling, I've made arrangements for something special tonight. Go below and change into the nicest thing you've brought."

"I was saving my one linen skirt for our overnight visit with Ian in Lima."

"Wear it tonight."

"What's going on?"

"Meet me on the front deck in thirty minutes, and you'll see."

Isabel came from below. The crew had congregated on the bow. They greeted Isabel with approving smiles. No one was smiling more than James.

He introduced her to the boat's captain. "My dear, this is Captain Beder Chavez Varas, and he's agreed to marry us."

James had made all the plans in Iquitos: he located a scribe in the town square who owned a Bible, and purchased a ticket for him on the same boat so the wedding proclamation could be completed by that evening; he conferred with the boat's cook, who prepared a traditional delicacy for the wedding feast; he bartered for the wedding ring — a hand-beaten tin band — with a small pocket sewing kit from the Hotel Bel-Air found in his toilet kit.

"I couldn't possibly share your cabin tonight without making an honest man out of myself first," said James.

The men removed their sweat-stained straw hats. Captain Varas improvised between equally inarticulate Portuguese and Spanish, occasionally looking solemnly at the Bible. The cabin boy stood as witness; his pet tamarin — tethered to the railing behind them — stopped chattering just as James placed the wedding band on Isabel's finger.

Hearts of palm spelled out *felice* on a platter of steamed yucca root. Isabel forced herself to eat monkey meat proudly presented by the cook. Serenaded by an odd-sounding, hand-carved flute, James asked Isabel to dance. He was still wearing his boots.

"If ever there was a time to put on those beautiful Belgian loafers of yours, it would be to dance at your wedding," suggested Isabel.

"I'm afraid a local tribesman is wearing them tonight," said James.

"What do you mean?" asked Isabel.

"I traded my shoes for your wedding present. . . . If you wait here, I'll get it."

James went below and quickly reappeared, hauling an enormous canvas bag that had previously stored bananas in the boat's galley.

"I had no idea how to wrap it . . . and it wasn't me who killed it," James admitted. "But the gesture is as male as you could ask for."

He pulled out the bloodied skin of an anaconda that measured seven feet from head to tail.

"You've passed my test," said Isabel after they slipped under the scratchy sheets of their cabin's single bed. "Now tell me how . . ."

James explained that shortly after the boat dropped anchor that afternoon, he spotted a local man dragging the just-killed snake at a remote bend of the river's edge. James went ashore and managed enough communication to negotiate a swap before returning to the boat for his Belgian loafers and a makeshift something that would enable him to transport his prize. By the time James found his way back to the village, the snake had been skinned and its meat shared among the tribe.

"Your test is responsible for making two men very happy tonight," said James as he kissed Isabel's eyes. "One man has in his possession the most beautiful shoes in New York — which he should save for special occasions, since they'll not last more than a few hours on the jungle floor. The other man has something far more satisfying than the shoes he once cherished . . . an admiring wife."

For the first time in her life, Isabel knew what her own happiness felt like. It was that night on the Amazon River. It was she with James. It was being both noun and verb.

Ian greeted James and Isabel at the Lima airport. They stayed overnight at the Grand Hotel Bolivar. Before parting company the next day, Ian gave Isabel a package.

"Please don't open it until I'm out of sight. I'm afraid I've been surrounded by livestock too long . . . I'm not very good with people."

Ian kissed his sister good-bye.

"I've included a note," he whispered in her ear. "Guess which hand wrote it?"

Wrapped in brown paper was a beautiful pair of silver spurs.

Dear James and Isabel,

If you use just one of the two spurs, it will only move a horse in circles no matter how hard you kick. But if you work both spurs together, the horse will take you wherever you wish to go.

Happy trails,

Ian

30

Several months after their not entirely legal marriage on the Amazon River, Isabel and James set the date for a civil ceremony on the Willoughby estate.

Rufus Simpson introduced himself formally to Mrs. Willoughby in a handwritten letter. She responded with one of her own and attached a bill for repairing and repainting the veranda where the ceremony would take place.

Mrs. Simpson's mental state had steadily improved since Isabel's hospital visit six months ago. Like a tolling bell, she announced herself in the wedding plans.

"Isabel, invitations are sent by the parents of the bride," pointed out Mrs. Simpson.

"But Mother, where would the replies be mailed? Father is in London for the next several months. What happens when the guests notice the invitation's return address belongs to a mental hospital? I don't think it sets an entirely comfortable tone."

"I'm sure we can make arrangements for the housekeeper to send the driver here with the replies," said Mrs. Simpson.

"Are you feeling confident about keeping track of it all?" asked Isabel.

"If I didn't, I wouldn't have suggested it," was her mother's sensible response.

Ian was to arrive from South America the morning of the wedding.

Mrs. Simpson arrived the day before with her husband and a three-day pass from the mental hospital. Not having met either of Isabel's parents, Mrs. Willoughby invited them to tea.

It started out promisingly. Mrs. Willoughby's first impression was a positive one: Mr. Simpson cut an imposing figure, and his wife was a lady. They certainly look the part, thought Mrs. Willoughby, visibly relieved. Odd that Isabel had been evasive about her family. By midway through the tea, Mrs. Willoughby concluded the Simpsons would be acceptable in-laws. That was before she asked Mrs. Simpson how she came to America. The question wasn't at all surprising. The answer left Mrs. Willoughby almost speechless.

"I came to this country after my father was killed in the war," said Mrs. Simpson. It was just the beginning of the answer. . . .

"I'm so sorry. Did he die fighting for the English?" asked Mrs. Willoughby, trying her best to pin down Mrs. Simpson's unidentifiable accent by geographical means.

"No. He was executed," said Mrs. Simpson.

This was the four-way stop sign where all parties, reaching the intersection at the same time, came to a full conversational halt and waited to see who among them would move through the cross-section first. James and his mother thought the explanation perhaps too painful for Mrs. Simpson — she seemed unwilling to take the lead. Their eyes turned to Mr. Simpson and Isabel. But father and daughter were just as spellbound as the Willoughbys by a dramatic story they, too, had yet to hear.

Mrs. Willoughby inched forward cautiously.

"How absolutely awful . . ."

As her words dangled in the air, Mrs. Willoughby's strained expression spoke of her increasing discomfort.

James knew of Mrs. Simpson's history of mental illness. He also knew of Mr. Simpson's self-made past. But, from what had just been said, it seemed there was even more to Isabel's background. James wasn't as enamored by convention as his mother. He was delighted to hear that, in addition to Isabel's originality, she apparently had a distant connection to wartime intrigue.

James sat forward, extremely interested. "Was he in the Resistance?" he asked Mrs. Simpson.

"Yes . . . but that wasn't the reason he was executed," she said.

Any one of them — Rufus, Isabel, Mrs. Willoughby, or James — could have asked the next question. It was destined for Mrs. Willoughby.

"I'm not sure I understand, Mrs. Simpson. What other reason could there have been?"

Tisza Simpson's completed answer was equivalent to reaching into her Birkin handbag, pulling out a grenade, calmly removing its pin, and rolling the explosive device on the parquet floor to the middle of the room.

"He was Jewish."

Whatever composure Mrs. Willoughby could call forth was spent entirely on the only thing she could think of saying.

"Excuse me while I see to the tea sandwiches."

Unlike his mother, James didn't excuse himself before walking out of the room. He retreated to the kitchen, where he found his mother scraping the deviled ham off the toast points.

"You should have mentioned this, James. . . . It really is *very* awkward," Mrs. Willoughby said through clenched teeth.

"Why would you think I knew?" asked James.

"You didn't?"

"Of course not. She has serious mental problems. That's all I was told."

"Dear God. . . . Are you telling me she's mentally unstable, *and* she's Jewish?"

"She's not Jewish unless her mother was," snapped James. He was furious with Isabel. How could she not have told him?

"You're just splitting hairs, and you know it," admonished his mother. "I suggest you consider the situation very carefully."

Mrs. Willoughby's next comment was spoken as though to herself, but it was just loud enough for her son to hear every word. "I was wondering why Isabel was so vague when I brought up the subject of her family."

Some words don't make an impact at the time they're spoken — they slip just beneath the skin's surface like a tiny splinter. What at first seems no more than an invisible irritant eventually becomes an infection. Regardless of whether she did so deliberately, Mrs. Willoughby called into question Isabel's honesty. She brushed up against her son ever so gently with the rough edge of doubt. It was just enough for a splinter.

31

Tisza Simpson's history was encrypted in elaborate and impossible-to-decipher codes.

Her husband and children understood the risk of delving too deeply. Asking would lead to knowing . . . unsettling the artificially calm surface. Until the wedding tea, none knew that one branch of Tisza's Viennese ancestors had migrated to Budapest and married into a distinguished Jewish family.

Even after the wedding tea, none would ever know the entire story — that Isabel's great-grandfather on her mother's maternal side was a decorated Austrian officer in World War I . . . and that her great-grandfather on her mother's paternal side founded the Hungarian Shipping Company. With the collapse of the Austro-Hungarian Empire, the two families intermarried. Assimilated generations managed to survive Communist oppression, plundering Romanian troops, and the authoritarian rule of an ultraconservative society. During World War II, Hungary fought primarily on the eastern front. When Isabel's grandfather, Lucien Karr, heard of the deportation of Jews in the provinces, he joined the Resistance in Budapest and sent his wife and daughter to safety among their Catholic relatives in Vienna.

A business partner of Lucien's father knew Lucien to be

Jewish by the fractional qualifier. He kept that dangerous secret; and, in doing so, risked his own life and that of his family during the occupation of Budapest. With the war drawing to a close — believing he'd survived the occupation because of the man's selfless act of protection — Lucien disclosed the whereabouts of a cache of buried family jewelry. He promised half of the hidden jewels out of gratitude.

As the Nazis tried in vain to fend off the Russian army, a newly sprouted Hungarian Fascist regime emerged. Unleashing their own evil during the chaotic last weeks of the war, they arrested antifascists, Jews, and any foreigners without papers. To lay claim to the entire treasure trove of jewels, the Hungarian who had protected Lucien Karr from the Nazis for four long years turned him in during the final few days of the war — not to a Nazi, but to a fellow Hungarian. Dragged from his house in the middle of the night, Lucien was ordered to line up with others on the Danube embankment facing the river. Shot in the back, he fell into the water and was washed away.

Lucien's wife suffered from a dangerous dementia. She was committed after trying to kill her daughter — Isabel's mother — who was raised by relatives in Vienna. Despite her scarred hands, Tisza was awarded a grant to Juilliard in New York, where she met and married Rufus Simpson.

During Tisza's own descent into madness, Rufus refused to consider separation or divorce. Rufus Simpson was a ruthless man, but he was a man of southern honor. Leaving his wife was out of the question. He would remain married to Tisza until she took her family's story to her own watery grave.

The afternoon Mrs. Simpson identified her long-deceased father as a Jew, James disappeared until his groom's dinner. Sitting the table's length from Isabel, James drank his way through what was meant to be a happy occasion. Isabel had no idea where James spent the night, or whether he would show up for the ceremony the next day.

At three in the morning, James appeared at the door to Isabel's bedroom.

"We need to talk," he said without coming into the room. "I'll be on the veranda."

Isabel slipped into her robe and slippers and stepped outside. It was chilly, and she began to shiver.

"Why didn't you tell me?"

"I didn't know," said Isabel. "And even if I did, it wouldn't have made any difference to me."

"But you knew it would have made a difference to me, and so you didn't tell me."

It was an unexpected and unfounded rebuke from the man she loved and thought she understood. Isabel was flabbergasted. "Are you suggesting I deceived you?"

"I'm suggesting you misled me with an omission."

"How could you possibly suggest such a thing! You knew of my mother's mental illness — why would her father's religion somehow be more important?"

"Both facts are important. The point is, you told me one and not the other. And it's not a religion, it's a race," insisted James before he walked away.

Returning to her room in a state of hurt and confusion, Isabel wrapped herself in a blanket and sat on the edge of the bed. At five in the morning, James reappeared. This time he came into the room.

"I can't tell you how ashamed of myself I am, Isabel. You'll forgive me, won't you?" he asked in a shaky voice.

"Of course I will," Isabel answered. She had been crying.

Gently pushing back hair strands stuck to her wet cheek, James said, "I needed one last chance to behave like a complete ass."

"The prospects of committing to one woman for a lifetime must unnerve the best of men," said Isabel.

". . . And no doubt makes the best of women think twice, if this is what the best of men have to offer them," jested James.

"I'm glad you've found your sense of humor again," Isabel said. "You'll need it when your mother meets my brother. I'm sure she'll think he's one more reason to be disappointed in your decision to marry me."

"Be patient with Mother until she comes around. . . . Listen, that reminds me, I thought you and your brother might like to do something together. Our neighbor has horses; I've made arrangements for both of you to take a ride before lunch."

"That was considerate of you, darling. . . . Now, please, try to get some rest, or you'll be a wreck tomorrow."

"This is tomorrow," James pointed out.

"My God . . . you're right. I guess I can't claim tomorrow will be another day. Get some sleep, James, and when you wake, we'll get married."

"And then? What then, my very own Isabel?"

"Then we'll give each other enough happiness for a lifetime."

James slept in the bedroom that had been his as a boy. Isabel fell into a shallow sleep while it was still dark, just as the birds began to sing. The dream came at false dawn . . . the dream of Isabel standing on the curb of an unknown street as James was driven away.

Isabel was the only one to welcome Ian in person. James was sleeping off the night before; Mr. and Mrs. Simpson were staying away from Mrs. Willoughby until their daughter's wedding that afternoon.

James's mother glared at Ian, who was eating a late breakfast with Isabel in the atrium. Just as Isabel had predicted, Mrs. Willoughby looked on him as another chilling indicator of the ill-conceived union between her son and Isabel.

"She's as subtle as iodine on a cut," was how Ian described Mrs. Willoughby.

"No one would be good enough for James," said Isabel. "I don't take it personally." But she did.

Two horses were tied to a fence directly in front of the tack house for the neighbor's stable. "Mother looks remarkably well for someone on a seventy-two-hour pass," said Ian as they bridled their mounts.

"Well, she certainly held her own yesterday. . . . Ian, did you ever think Mother had Jewish ancestors?"

"Does she?"

"She told us during tea. Mrs. Willoughby looked horrified . . . as though by marrying her son, I'm watering down the Willoughby bloodline."

"The ruder bark to the kinder tree," quipped Ian as he gave Isabel a leg up on her horse and then tightened its cinch. "Did you know a horse deliberately bloats its girth as soon as it sees you walking toward it with a saddle? They're not as stupid as their reputation."

"Exactly what does that mean?" asked Isabel. "Not the horse's girth — I get that — and I don't think them stupid, by the way; but now that you've explained their maniacal girth trick, I'll never trust them again. What did you mean by that expression? And which one am I, the bark or the tree?"

"The best cattle have always come from crossbreeding," said Ian while adjusting his stirrups. "James's mother should be thanking you. They've probably been inbreeding for years. If you hadn't shown up, the next generation of Willoughbys would have been hemophiliacs or imbeciles."

"I'm sure that's the kind of reassurance Mrs. Willoughby is waiting to hear," said Isabel. "Be sure and explain it to her just that way."

They rode across the road and into an open field. "So, did you ever know?" Isabel asked again.

"Izzie, I haven't *any* idea about Mother . . . never have. She wasn't real to me. Was she to you?"

"Occasionally . . . in moments."

"Tell me about the moments," Ian said.

Isabel smiled. "Well, I think the most fabulous moment was when I watched her slap a stranger in the face."

"What brought that on?"

"He took her parking space . . . she insisted he give it back . . . he called her a bitch, and she slapped him. I saw it all."

Ian pressed for details. "And . . . ?"

"She was so completely sure of herself. This jerk of a man did the wrong thing and refused to admit it. Mother tried civility. He responded with a vulgarity. She slapped him with all the force of her conviction and her ring . . . it left the most enormous gash on the side of his face. And afterward, when she returned to our car, she didn't have a hair out of place."

Ian was impressed. "Wow . . . Are there any more you can remember?"

When Isabel thought further, the expression on her open face closed abruptly.

"Just before you take your own life must be its most real moment," she said, more to herself than to Ian.

Ian halted his horse and loosened the reins, allowing it to graze. Isabel did the same. She looked at her brother.

"You saw it, didn't you?" he asked.

"I tried stopping her," said Isabel.

On the morning she was to be wed, after countless years of isolating her brother from the truth, Isabel finally admitted to it.

"I had one terrifying moment of knowing Mother was real, and then she was expunged," she said. "They followed my bloody tracks to the bathroom where I was hiding. I was covered in Mother's blood, so I was told to stand in the bathtub. They hosed me down . . . as if I were part of the incriminating evidence. By afternoon, whatever was Mother had been wiped clean."

They were quiet for what felt like a long time before Ian spoke.

"Remember our childhood fables?"

"I regaled James with *The Chronicles of Akakor* on the Amazon," said Isabel.

"So, can you tell me who the patron saint of England is?" asked Ian.

"Of course I can — he was your favorite," said Isabel. "You pretended the top half of you was Saint George and the bottom half was his horse — that way you could brandish your sword and rear up at the same time."

"Saint George wasn't English." Ian's matter-of-fact statement was flattened by the disappointment of someone taking the information it conveyed personally.

"What the hell was he?" asked Isabel.

"He came from southeast Europe, and he died in Palestine."

"You're kidding."

"No, I'm not kidding. I couldn't take two steps at British boarding school without falling over an image of him on horseback slaying the dragon. He turned out to be a foot soldier, for God's sake."

Isabel was just as amazed as Ian was resentful to have been misled by the legend during all the years he reenacted it as a boy. "What a scam," she said with palpable disgust.

"How did he end up personifying Christian chivalry?" Ian continued complaining. "And why put him on a horse when he never owned one?"

"Damned if I know. Who falsified his records?" asked Isabel.

"What difference does it make?" asked Ian before illustrating his point. "Mother probably has strains of all of Eastern Europe in her blood. Why would it matter what part belongs where?"

"I suppose you're right," said Isabel, gathering her reins and pulling her horse up from grazing.

"I'd be far more concerned about Mrs. Willoughby," joked Ian. "Despite her undiluted bloodline, she looks menacing . . . a kind of darkly Freudian Mrs. Danvers. My advice is that you and James spend as little time at Mandalay as possible."

Isabel laughed in a way Ian hadn't heard since they were children.

"I'll race you to the other side of the field," Isabel said before she spurred her horse into a full gallop.

That afternoon, James and Isabel were wed.

James was hung over.

Isabel's mother stared in the fixed distance to some other place.

Mrs. Willoughby oozed disapproval.

Mr. Simpson resented standing on a veranda for which he had been invoiced.

The only person in the small wedding party who radiated certainty was the bride. Isabel gave herself to every word of the vows. Two men stood by her side. One was Ian, anchoring her to all that was decent. The other was John, wearing the tie she bought for him in Paris.

145

★ ★ ★

On their first anniversary, James wrote of his happiness:

> Dear John,
>
> Isabel and I enjoy each other so much, we fear it's a setup for something unthinkable that would part us. Today has been a joyous anniversary. We've reminisced about how she spotted my piece in the Sunday *Times,* and you warned her, "He's trouble." We've laughed over the disastrous first lunch, after which you asked, "What did I tell you?" . . . And the dinner at Sousceyrac when I attempted to show my potential, and you told her, "Take a chance."
>
> Plainly, you've been a part of what seems to me that rarest and greatest opportunity, a happy marriage. Thank you, dear sponsor, for Isabel.

There would be nothing capricious about how the fates plotted Isabel's story. The carefully chosen words in James's letter would one day be mocked with ruthless irony even the most cynical author might have found heart enough to withhold.

32

Marriage was good for Isabel. It reached in and opened her up.

Her sadness faded into a past she was finally able to let die a quiet death. Her reserve gave way to spontaneity, and she grew fond of laughing.

Anyone who saw them together could see it. Isabel and James were transfixed by one another. They shared the same dry wit. They possessed the same refined sensibility. They understood that, in their lucky case, love and sex were coincidentally one and the same. They were alike in so very many ways, Isabel took for granted that James would feel as she did about responsibility. When James's chronic lack of responsibility was impossible to deny, Isabel had the idea that she must not say too much. In the manner she was raised, it was always better to say too little than too much. Isabel was sure James would find his way toward obligation once they had a child.

After marvel, after delight, after pride, Isabel pregnant became a woman of another purpose. It was then that she realized James's sense of obligation would not be joining her own . . . not even by way of a child.

When Isabel asked, James stated unequivocally, "I have no intention of buying life insurance."

"For God's sake, why not?"

"It's like betting against your own life."

"Well, what about a will?"

"If it's that important to you, then you do it for me."

"I can't draw up your will, James. You'll need to give instructions to an attorney. . . . I thought Robert Gallagher."

"Just tell him it all goes to you, along with the Willoughby estate, assuming my mother has gone. You mustn't ever sell any part of the land. Promise me, Izzie."

"Of course I won't. And, if I go before you —"

"What makes you so sure *you'll* be the lucky one?" interrupted James.

"No life support if something happens to me."

"God, Isabel, what a macabre conversation."

"I know, but it's just something we should take care of now."

"I'll sign whatever you want, and we'll never discuss it again."

Isabel made arrangements with a friend, Robert Gallagher, who was the managing partner for a white-shoe law firm. James agreed to meet her in the law office on a weekday afternoon. Isabel, along with a lawyer from estate planning and two witnesses, waited for over an hour. Robert was told by his secretary that nothing seemed to be progressing. He got up from his desk and walked down the hall to the conference room.

"Even if James ever gets around to signing the necessary papers, God forbid the time ever comes, he'll forget to show up at your bedside to pull the plug," said Robert. "I suggest you designate someone else, or you'll be hooked up to machinery for years. It'll drain away your assets."

"Can I appoint you?"

"It's usually family. What about your brother?"

"He's out in the middle of nowhere."

"Jesus, Isabel . . ."

"Well, will you?"

"I guess I'll have to, given a brother who'll never be found . . . and the flaky husband," Robert muttered.

"What I really need is a creative change," insisted James, who didn't wish to discuss his no-show at the law offices.

"Well, what interests you?" asked Isabel.

"I think I'd like to write a novel," he answered.

"Why can't you do both — your assigned pieces and a novel?"

"Because I just can't."

"What about a column?"

"I don't want deadlines in my life."

"James, how do you propose earning a living?"

"Don't worry, Donna Isabel. One day I'll be rich."

"You make it sound like a fait accompli. Why assume we'll be rich?" asked Isabel.

"Because I've never imagined my life without a great deal of money," James said.

It was the kind of bizarre pronouncement more likely to have been made by an idiot savant than a rational adult.

Isabel believed James had a gift. He had engaging ideas to express, and the imagination to express them with originality. James told Isabel he wanted a great deal of money. Isabel was sure he'd make a great deal of money if that was what he wanted. After all, she thought, he was far more talented than the financially successful writers she published.

One is never as deaf as when one chooses not to hear. Isabel wasn't listening to James's words.

★   ★   ★

"Now that you're expecting a baby, there's really no more need for us to have anything to do with one another." Mrs. Simpson's savage rejection came over the phone. Isabel listened to the dial tone after her mother hung up. She's right . . . no more need, Isabel said to herself. No more need for reasons, or for answers. I have a husband . . . and soon we'll have a child. They're my only reason now . . . and all the answers I'll ever need.

When Isabel and James were told they were expecting a boy, Isabel phoned the person who'd predicted it thirteen years before.

"You'll be his godmother?" asked Isabel.

"I've been waiting," said Monina. "What will you call him?"

"Willoughbys rotate their male names."

"Do any appeal to you?"

"No."

"Well, give him his own damn name," insisted Monina. "Why should he get a preassigned one?"

"It's terribly important to James's mother," said Isabel.

"Forget the mother . . . she sounds like a nightmare. Tell James it's simple: he gets the foreskin decision, and you get to choose the name."

As she filled out the birth certificate form, Isabel remembered the panache the name foretold when she first spotted it in a Trollope novel. She said it aloud and could almost taste the name by its cadence. The minister at All Saints Church on Fifth Avenue took care to enunciate "Burgo Simpson Willoughby" as he christened Isabel and James's son.

Isabel was eager to describe Burgo's christening to John, who'd been too frail to travel to New York. She allowed her phone call an irrationally persistent number of rings. There would be no answer. John had disconnected his answering machine before going to sleep that afternoon. He knew he would never wake.

John didn't leave a note. If the medics had taken a moment to look at the book they moved off John's chest, they'd have seen what he was reading before he died. And if they'd noticed the page where the book lay open, they'd have known that the last words of his life were from T. S. Eliot:

> Home is where one starts from. As we grow older
> The world becomes stranger, the pattern more complicated
> Of dead and living. Not the intense moment
> Isolated, with no before or after,
> But a lifetime burning in every moment . . .

33

It was as if God scrolled down a menu of chromosomes and chose DNA from various genetic columns.

Burgo inherited James's charm with women, Isabel's single-mindedness, Rufus's competitive streak, and Tisza's love of music.

When Burgo was able to sit up, Isabel put him on the floor and played a recording of *Peter and the Wolf.* The baby lunged forward in his sitting position. Realizing he hadn't transported himself any closer to the source of the music, Burgo gestured wildly. Isabel moved him nearer to the stereo speaker. Leaning into the symphonic sound, Burgo's face evoked a kaleidoscopic range of pleasure.

Every night before Isabel read the baby to sleep, James played a new concerto or aria for Burgo.

"I put on *Pictures at an Exhibition,*" enthused James, "and the boy's changing expressions took on just that . . . pictures at an exhibition. He's the best possible entertainment. Tomorrow night I'm trying *Madame Butterfly* on him."

"You certainly will not," Isabel insisted. "It will only upset him. You're like a sinister rewrite of *The Music Man.* No more experiments, James, I mean it."

New York is a city where recommendation letters are a prerequisite for toddlers who are interviewed before applying to a nursery school that charges $24,000 for three half-days a week. Isabel and James thought there might be an alternative course for Burgo. They kept him home. It was a kitchen appliance — not a standardized test — that charted Burgo's intelligence.

Burgo spent the last few weeks of his first year in his high chair, but he wasn't especially interesting in eating. The high chair provided an unencumbered view of the dishwasher, which Burgo watched with unbroken attention. Isabel assumed his fascination had to do with the variety of noises the machine emitted when it graduated from one cycle to the next. The afternoon he took his first steps, with a gait that swayed him back and forth like a small dinghy caught in choppy waters, Burgo headed purposely toward the dishwasher as if it were a safe dock. Grabbing on to the counter's ledge to steady himself, he punched various buttons in their correct order before starting the machine: *energy save, heavy wash, low temperature, rinse, air dry, on.*

"Did you see that?" Isabel asked James.

"It has to be luck," he said.

"Let's find out. Take him out of the room, and I'll scramble the dials."

When James opened the kitchen door and stepped aside, Burgo made a beeline to the machine and repeated the sequential task, despite the fact that Isabel had jumbled its controls into chronological disarray.

"Jesus . . . he must have been watching from the high chair all this time," said James. "We'd better keep him away from circuit breakers."

The simplest conceit became ingenious grounds for Burgo to organize the variables of his small universe. After breakfast one morning, Burgo insisted the housekeeper open the refrigerator door so he could study what was inside. As Isabel was rushing through the kitchen, late getting to the office, she found her son — wearing a T-shirt and diaper — standing in front of the open refrigerator.

"Elvita, if Burgo wishes to commune with the refrigerator, please make sure he's wearing a sweater . . . and try to limit him to five minutes, or the food will spoil."

Burgo stood in front of the open refrigerator for his allotted five minutes muffled in his outdoor coat for three days. For three consecutive days of his five-minute time allowance, he looked intently but touched nothing. Until the fourth day . . .

Isabel was dressing; James was shaving. Elvita knocked on the bedroom door.

"Mrs. Isabel, come quick. Burgo is changing the icebox."

Isabel had no idea what "changing the icebox" meant, but she guessed from the lack of panic in Elvita's voice that there was no imminent danger. Still, they hurried into the kitchen — Isabel in her slip and James with shaving cream on his face — and watched as their son methodically separated the foods he knew his father liked from those his mother preferred. Anything green was placed on one side for her; the white wine was placed on the other, for James. The next day, Burgo demoted his father's items into the bottom compartment, away from his own chocolate pudding and his mother's vegetables, both of which were advanced to the highest shelf he could reach.

"Frankly, Isabel, I don't trust the boy."

"What a terrible thing to say, even in jest," said Isabel.

"He's been around before. I can tell by the way he stares at me."

"He's inherited that from his mother. When I was little, my stare always unnerved the adults."

"It's not just his stare. . . . There's something else about him . . . he's too sure of himself for a baby."

"Don't be silly," said Isabel.

"What about the fact he never sucked his thumb or used a pacifier? What kind of baby is that?" asked James.

"Ours," said Isabel.

"It doesn't bother you that he's already assumed command of every piece of mechanical equipment in this apartment? Do you know what he's done with my computer?"

"No, James, what has he done with your computer?"

"I'll tell you exactly what he's done. He's created his own."

"His own what?"

"Files, files . . . the boy has created his own files. The fact he doesn't know how to spell hasn't slowed him down. He's done it phonetically."

"Well, you should be pleased your son is so clever," said Isabel. She was taken aback to hear about Burgo's computer initiative, but decided any reaction would only encourage James, who was still at it.

"And another thing . . . Anyone can see he wants you to himself. It's like living with a deposed South American dictator," said James. "I think we should get rid of him before he learns to talk."

"I won't hear any more. . . . It's not funny."

"Who's being funny? God only knows what will happen to me when the child is capable of communicating. I'll probably be hauled off on trumped-up charges he's been plotting for months."

In truth, James knew that what he had right now was the sum total of a happiness he couldn't have imagined before. He counted his blessings every morning. Suspicious that pride would attract misfortune, James selfishly held on to his contentment without boasting of it to anyone.

Moving with ease through their charmed existence, Isabel and James thought of each other in the same magical way the world thought of them. They were deeply, madly, irreversibly in love. Undiluted happiness came in the company of one another and Burgo. But it didn't take long before Isabel began to realize that their marvelous three-person drama — no matter how chicly written — had an unscripted character waiting in the wings. It was James's drinking . . . and it was prepared to enter stage right or stage left at any time.

Statisticians, when graphing charts, establish a baseline in order to compare information and draw conclusions. James's baseline — his personality without drink — was willfully eccentric . . . which made it easier for Isabel to believe James's drinking self was just an extension of his uncensored, sober self. But ever so often, circumstances measured the distance between James and reality.

"Darling, is today the weekend?" James asked after phoning Isabel at her office.

"My dear, your call was routed through a receptionist and then my secretary. Do you really think we'd all be in the office on a weekend?"

"Oh, good . . . that must mean the banks are open. Thank God one of us knows the day. I'm wild about you, sweetie, regardless of where I happen to be in space and time."

There was nothing typical about James when he was sober; not surprisingly, he wasn't a typical drinker. Drink didn't slow his hair-trigger wit, dull his pitch-perfect ear, or cloud his clear eye — all three remained at the service of his unique sense of humor. Drink never resulted in acrimony between them. And so Isabel did everything to ignore James's drinking when she could, and to give it a wide berth when she needed. Like Lewis Carroll's poem about the Jabberwock, James's drinking was the menacing creature in another place. It was in the moment, but never really there; it was ominously possible, but never actually threatening. That's what Isabel allowed herself to believe during the first several years of her marriage . . . until she came home one day and realized the menacing creature was no longer in another place.

34

There was no more inheritance left.

James appeased Isabel by agreeing to writing assignments. The *New York Times Magazine* asked him to profile Paul Mellon, whose autobiography was soon to be published. The first of what were to be several interviews had been scheduled on a Friday afternoon. Isabel came home from the office to be greeted by Elvita, who was meant to have left hours ago. James hadn't shown up at the designated time.

Later that night, the front door opened as Isabel was putting Burgo to bed. Her first reaction was relief.

"James, I'm in Burgo's room. Is everything all right?"

James loomed at the doorway of Burgo's small room. Burgo sensed his father's transformation. Instead of greeting James with his usual grin, the boy started to wail. Without taking off his overcoat, James sat down and began to weep.

Simultaneously called on by son and husband, Isabel had no idea which of the two she should comfort first. She tried talking to James above Burgo's frightened crying, "Tell me what's happened!"

"I don't know," was all he could manage.

"Why don't you go into the other room and let me get Burgo down, then I'll make you a cup of tea."

By the time Isabel calmed Burgo, James had passed out on the bed. He thrashed about, ensnaring himself in twisted sheets like a large fish caught in a net. Isabel curled up on the settee and covered herself with a comforter. Just at the point of drifting off to sleep, she was awoken by the incongruous sound of running water. James was drawing a bath at one o'clock in the morning. Isabel had never known James to take baths, only showers. He took six baths before daybreak.

While James was taking his second, Isabel talked to him from the other side of the locked bathroom door. "Don't you want me to keep you company?"

"No! I need to do this on my own."

"I'm worried, please let me in."

James had the shakes. "Go away, Isabel."

"At least let me call the doctor," begged Isabel.

"No, I can do this."

"But I can't," said Isabel in tears. She was afraid. James was too. Before that night, he couldn't have imagined the physical pain of coming off a bender.

At seven o'clock in the morning, Isabel — exhausted by stress and lack of sleep — strapped Burgo into his stroller.

"I realize it's a bit early for a stroll in the park, but your father needs some time to himself," said Isabel as they entered Central Park by way of Engineer's Gate, its East Ninetieth Street entrance, a few blocks from their brownstone apartment. "Daddy doesn't seem to be feeling well. I think we should give him some time to fall back asleep, so let's stay out in the fresh air as long as possible."

Isabel and Burgo made two trips around the reservoir on the bridle path. They lingered over hot chocolate in a Madison Avenue café. They read TinTin at the Corner Bookstore. Finally, at eleven o'clock, there was no choice but to return to the apartment. Burgo's wet diaper had soaked his pants.

Isabel slipped into the apartment as unobtrusively as possible. The door to the master bedroom was closed. Thank God he's sleeping, thought Isabel. She took Burgo to his room and removed his saturated diaper.

"Urine boy," she said to him playfully. "I'll think we'll hold off on another diaper for a bit so your bottom can recover from this morning's high dose of ammonia."

Wearing nothing but his polo shirt, Burgo trotted to the CD player and stood in front of it expectantly, waiting for Isabel to make a musical selection.

"Well, all right, pet. But no brass instruments . . . let's find something with woodwinds or a gentle sonata." Isabel flipped through the CDs. "What about Satie?"

She placed Burgo on a sheepskin he called "Bah" and settled into a comfortable armchair opposite him to read a manuscript. When Burgo fell asleep on his sheepskin, Isabel decided to look in on James. She opened the bedroom door slowly so as not to disturb him.

James had vanished.

He was in the habit of keeping his passport on top of the bedroom bureau. After nearly five years of marriage, James still tucked it into his inside breast pocket each morning before leaving the apartment.

"Why walk around with a passport? Are you planning a foreign excursion before dinner?" Isabel once asked lightheartedly.

"You never know," had been his answer.

So much about James was "you never know." The three words were what Isabel liked best about him. They suggested life as a series of adventures. But the same words served as fair warning.

While she waited for her husband to return from an undisclosed location, it occurred to Isabel that James could be anywhere. Isabel and Burgo were not included in whatever it was that had happened to James. James had left. Wherever he'd gone was away from them. There was no guarantee James would include them in whatever was next. For Isabel to admit to that . . . for her to know the awful actuality of it . . . was to feel the worst kind of loneliness.

He phoned that night.

"James, say you're all right."

"I decided to go home."

"What do you mean by 'home'? That's what you've just left . . . and when you left it, you left your son and your wife, who's been terribly worried about you all day."

"I'll be back soon. How is Burgo?"

Isabel reined in anger and hid the disappointment, but she couldn't contain her apprehension. Why would he leave without at least writing a note? And why head back to his childhood home? On the other hand, reasoned Isabel, James had been in a desperate state. Perhaps he'd find his bearings sooner if he did so apart from her and Burgo. It'll be just a short time, Isabel reassured herself. Best to be supportive. She wouldn't criticize. She'd wait to hear from him rather than phone . . . that way he wouldn't feel she was checking up.

Four days after James left, Isabel received his letter.

Isabella,

To pass from the light of our Eden into the black hole of self-loathing is what the Italians call "chiaroscuro." I promise to find my way back.

Know my heart is and will always be yours.

Two weeks later, James reappeared just as he'd departed —
unannounced and without explanation. All that mattered to Isabel
was that he was back, and he was no longer drinking. She was too
grateful to ask questions.

35

Like James in his infancy, Burgo was slow to speak.

That didn't prevent him from squealing in the delighted anticipation of bedtime stories.

Children's tales often begin with travesty. Certainly it is so with *The Adventures of Babar*. Babar, an elephant, is orphaned when "an evil hunter" shoots his mother. Having witnessed the murder, baby Babar, understandably traumatized, runs from the crime scene.

It was difficult for Isabel to refrain from editorializing after reading each page out loud, but she'd wait for her son's reaction before putting forth her own.

Burgo responded to the illustration of the evil hunter by saying "uh-oh!" — and Isabel added, "Look at all that khaki, Burgo. I say he's been outfitted entirely at Hollanders. I bet the evil hunter is English, and Babar's mother ends up as a plaque on the main hall of his Wiltshire estate."

Isabel continued reading. . . .

Alone and lost, Babar wanders out of the jungle and into what looked to be a resort town, where he meets a woman who's identified only by her age and sizable fortune.

"Little Babar has left the jungle and somehow has managed

to land on Worth Avenue in Palm Beach," said Isabel before reading on.

Babar moves in with "the old lady who is rich," as the book
describes her. Shortly after settling in with the wealthy woman,
Babar seems to mature at alarming speed because, four pages into
the book, a tailor is fitting him for a waistcoat. Isabel applauded
the formality of Babar's attire. She was less enthusiastic about the
brazenness of his shopping spree. Not only did "the rich woman"
purchase Babar's suits, she made a gift of a red convertible. It was
shamefully obvious Babar had no problem with the fact that, for
all practical purposes, he was being kept.

Before Isabel commented on Babar's trip to the tailor, Burgo
furrowed his brow in a studious knot of concentration and expressed his own editorial point.

"Papi," he said.

"The elephant's name is *Babar,* my sweet," Isabel corrected
gently.

"Papi," Burgo insisted.

Isabel flipped the pages backward to the book's introduction
of Babar; but Burgo didn't refer to him as "Papi." She turned
every page, and still no reference to Babar as "Papi" . . . until she
arrived at the page where Babar was being attended to by the tailor. It was only then that Burgo pointed to the elephant and said
"Papi." Burgo continued identifying Babar as Papi when, on the
next page, Babar was trying on spats; and on the next, when the
woman was paying for the expensive red car.

At the time she was reading the Babar story, Burgo had yet
to call Isabel or James by any name. It finally dawned on Isabel
that Burgo was calling James "Papi," rather than "Daddy." James
was elegant by nature and stylish by design. Isabel thought that

perhaps James might have taken Burgo along with him to his tailor without mentioning it to her.

Regardless of Burgo's reasoning, "Papi" became Burgo's name for James. It would be the only child's word incorporated in what was to become his son's otherwise adult vocabulary.

Burgo was just about the age children enter grade school when James announced he intended to leave New York.

"I need a change," is how James put it. "I want to write a screenplay."

"But James, if you want to try some other form of writing, surely you could do it from New York. Why a move to the West Coast?"

"Because this coast isn't working for me anymore. I'm through with New York."

"I run a company, darling. I just can't pack up and move."

"Maybe you could take a sabbatical," suggested James.

"James, I'm a book publisher, not an academic. Nothing like that's available to someone in my position. I oversee a staff."

"I'm stalled here," said James. "I need something different. I'm afraid if I stay, I'll start to drink again."

Isabel dared not argue with those words. She would find a way to move them to Los Angeles, even if it meant commuting.

Monina had long ago come to the conclusion that James's God-given talent suggested more than it accomplished. She kept that opinion to herself when Isabel phoned with the news that they'd be spending time in L.A. so James might pursue screenwriting.

"Your husband can take care of himself," she said. "But I don't want the boy anywhere near the movie industry."

"He'll be in school, Monina, not pitching story ideas on the Paramount lot," Isabel said.

"Well, I need to see him before you decamp. I suppose that means he'll have to bring the two of you."

A whaling captain in the late 1700s had built the house Monina bought when she sold *Catch-22*. It sat on a beautiful tree-lined street with its back to the sound. One of its past owners had cultivated a small walled garden between the house and the water. During forty years of an illustrious career, Monina left her home only for her office in the city. She spoke with a few locals in the tiny hamlet, which had a single general store and church. Monina's home was her seawall. She guarded her privacy by not allowing any visitors past its front door.

As she had clairvoyantly foretold, Monina loved Burgo as her own. Burgo returned Monina's adoration. "Old Man" is what Monina called him.

"Isabel and James, you have the front room," said Monina when they arrived. "And you, Old Man, where would you like to sleep?"

"If we sleep in the same room, you can tell me tales," Burgo answered.

36

L.A. is a manmade city, not the result of a confluence of resources. That could explain why — unlike New York — L.A. doesn't pass judgment on those who show up to reinvent themselves.

Isabel took two weeks away from work in New York to settle the family in L.A. before she began a weekly commute from one to the other. James went ahead to scout for a house.

"I've found it," he trumpeted over the phone. "A Richard Neutra house on Mulholland Drive. Wait until you see the view, sweetie, it's positively aerial."

"James, we don't always have to find the most stylish way of going about things. Renting a Neutra house sounds wildly extravagant."

"We're in L.A., darling. I say we leave behind our Aesthetic Movement period and set a course toward postmodern clarity. This is just what we both need, an entirely different look."

"How are we affording our different look, James?"

"Don't worry. I've taken it on a six-month lease. Just enough time for me to sell the first draft for a movie that will make me rich."

"I don't know . . . it seems financially reckless. There must be other ways," Isabel repeated.

"Of course there are other ways. There are always other ways. But this is the most fun way. What would be the point otherwise?"

"I can think of a few. One is that we're carrying the rent in New York at the same time."

"If it's practicality you're after, you'll be pleased to know that I've thought it all out in that rigorously linear way you do. I don't know how you manage. I found it completely exhausting to be so logical. Anyway, I stayed on message, as you business people say, and I can tell you precisely why this house makes sense."

"I'm all ears."

"We need Elvita."

"Yes . . . ?"

"The one thing that makes it possible for you to commute until I make a fortune is Elvita," explained James.

"And . . . ?"

"And how can she possibly turn down six months in a guest house overlooking a pool that's right out of a David Hockney painting?"

Elvita didn't know who David Hockney was; nor did she know how to swim or drive. The house was balanced on the spine of Benedict Canyon, at least twenty minutes from a market or playground. James's proposition was expensive and impractical, but he sounded his happiest in years. It would be a new beginning, thought Isabel.

L.A. assigns its hopefuls a winning divide between those who place phone calls and those who receive them. How and when you do either defines your status and is often responsible for your income. A phone call from Larry Berg granted Burgo last-minute admission to the otherwise impossible-to-get-into Beverly Hills grade school.

Larry Berg was the head of a major studio whose movies resulted in the kind of consistent box office success that propelled him from one lucrative contract renewal to the next. In an industry of revolving doors, Larry wasn't going anywhere. That made him the most impressive kind of incoming call.

Isabel met Larry as a result of selling performance rights to a book she'd published several years back. Larry had been impressed with Isabel's negotiating skills. Not far below her elegant surface was the cutting instinct to win. Larry liked that. He decided he wanted that on his side. He took Isabel to dinner at Morton's and offered more income for one year's work with him than she'd make in five of book publishing. Isabel responded in a way with which he was unfamiliar . . . she turned him down and became his friend.

There was only one acceptable grade school in town, Larry told Isabel when she phoned. It was the one his daughter attended.

"Wait one minute . . . I'm jumping on the other line," he interrupted.

"Can you describe the school to me?" asked Isabel when he got back on with her.

"It's the one he should be in. And besides, I've already made arrangements."

"What do you mean, you've already made arrangements? What arrangements?"

"I've already made the call. He's in. I've got CAA on the other line. Be sure and let me know if you need anything else."

Isabel realized she was no longer in New York City when she was told that parents of new students were expected to drop off earthquake kits a week before the start of school. Required items included three days' supply of water, dried food, and clothes, along with a letter reassuring Burgo . . . presumably to be read by another adult, with the aid of the flashlight also included in his kit.

Isabel deliberately brought Burgo on her search for the kit's items, hoping it might put the idea of earthquakes in psychological perspective for both of them. Burgo thought of it as an adventure, as if they were on a kind of final treasure hunt. Isabel forfeited all reason and convinced herself a fault line would swallow her son. Her anxiety increased with each item dutifully crossed off the list as she and Burgo cruised the wide aisles of Trader Joe's, an enormous and eclectically stocked general store.

They loaded the trunk of the car. "This is how those survivalists in Idaho must shop," Isabel told Burgo. "The only things missing are a manifesto and the ammo."

37

Cars in L.A. are moving tax returns. Year and model are coded status symbols. License plates abbreviate drivers' identities with clues to personal, professional, and sexual characteristics.

Cars in L.A. contain interior lives for all to see. If you're stopped at a light on a double-lane street and look at the adjacent car, you might spot a woman taking the momentary opportunity to pluck her eyebrows in her rearview mirror; or a man, red in the face, spraying spittle as he mutely screams at unseen frustrations.

Most people driving from one location to the next in L.A. are lost in their interior-car world. But on a rare occasion, what is seen from the inside looking out becomes an integral part of life looking forward. That's what happened to Isabel at the corner of La Brea and Sunset.

Returning home from their earthquake-kit mission, Isabel caught a red light. While waiting for it to change, she learned almost everything she would need to know about her son. Sitting in a rented Miata convertible — small and low to the ground — Isabel and Burgo watched as a man in a wheelchair pushed himself at an excruciatingly slow pace across the street. The green light in his favor was already flashing an impatient yellow, and he wasn't yet at middle ground.

"He's very brave," Isabel said to Burgo, the words catching in her throat.

When the man was directly in front of them, Burgo and Isabel saw that he had absolutely no legs. There wasn't even a suggestion of legs where they were meant to be. Isabel knew that before the man made it to the other side of the street, she would cry.

"He proves his bravery every day in the simplest act of trying to get across the street," Isabel said.

"I know, I know, Mommy," said Burgo, without taking his eyes off the man. "But I have a question . . ."

Isabel waited for what she was sure would be Burgo's contemplative question about the human condition.

"How did that man get to the store to buy his wheelchair?" Burgo wanted to know.

Isabel's foot didn't move off the brake when the light turned green. Only when angry horns bellowed did she drive through the intersection.

Isabel pulled the car into a parking lot and turned off the ignition.

"What did you mean about the man and his wheelchair?" she asked.

Burgo repeated himself, "I don't understand how the man got to the store to buy the wheelchair."

There it was . . . the difference between the two of them. Regardless of how well-calibrated her brain, Isabel was a romantic at heart. On the opposite side of sentiment was her son, a staunch reductionist.

Isabel broke into laughter.

"Burgo, you've provided pathos in the most unlikely way."

"That's no answer," he said pragmatically.

"Well, sweetheart, I really don't know how he got himself to the wheelchair store."

"I don't think his wife drove him," suggested Burgo. "I think he must have had an old wheelchair he traded in for a new one. That would explain it."

"Why don't you think his wife drove him?"

"I don't think he has a wife. On the other hand, he might have a wife, but he's lost his wedding band."

Isabel's flabbergasted face dropped its jaw.

"Why are we waiting here?" asked Burgo.

"We're not," Isabel said as she turned the car key. "Let's go home and assemble your earthquake kit."

After packing the steel earthquake box, Isabel sat at her desk and tried to visualize the bleak circumstances that would require its final inclusion . . . her letter to Burgo. She decided to keep it short.

> My dear one,
>
>   Don't worry. Mommy and Papi will come as soon as we can. Remember how much we love you, and you will be safe.

But Isabel knew better. She knew that if there were a disaster her son managed to survive but she didn't, whatever she wrote would prove false. Burgo mistrusted promises that lay beyond reality. He wouldn't believe his mother's reassuring words, no matter how she phrased them. So Isabel placed a photograph in with the letter before sealing its envelope. It pictured Isabel, her arms around Burgo, with James standing behind the two, his arms tightly encircling them. They were all three laughing.

Before she returned to New York, Isabel dropped off Burgo's earthquake kit at the school and set up a house account at the local market. And then it began.

Isabel ricocheted like a pinball between the unrelenting demands of two coasts. Every Thursday she worked through dinner and left from her office to the airport for a late-night flight. Isabel would arrive in L.A. and grab what sleep she could before getting up in time for breakfast with James and Burgo. The rest of the day was spent on the phone to New York. Isabel was on an overnight flight Sunday, crossing the width of the country — this time in the opposite direction — arriving Monday morning in time to cab directly to the office or a breakfast meeting.

The Friday before Burgo began school, Isabel and James attended parents' night. Fellow parents were seated in a small circle. Isabel couldn't help but notice an unsettling similarity among breasts and teeth.

"They all have surgically frozen expressions. . . . How are you suppose to know what they're thinking when you can't read their faces?" Isabel whispered to James.

The headmistress introduced herself and then proceeded with a "this-is-an-important-threshold-for-your-child" litany. Isabel allowed her brain to wander off-site until she heard something that didn't quiet make sense . . . apparently, the children were offered certain dolls during playtime.

Isabel's face, not rendered into a lightbulb smoothness by the scalpel, was able to covey all aspects of her confusion to everyone in the seated circle.

"I don't quite understand," she said.

"We want our students to appreciate the fact that the world is made up of people of all races everywhere," the headmistress explained in a serious tone.

"'Everywhere' doesn't seem to include Beverly Hills," whispered Isabel to James, who had anticipated an evening of sheer boredom and was just beginning to realize it might become good dinner theater.

"If the headmistress learned correct sentence structure, the children might have a better chance to appreciate the goodwill she's hoping to inspire," he said to Isabel, sotto voce.

"I still don't see the point of the dolls," Isabel reiterated out loud.

"There are no minority students, and so we encourage the children to play with the dolls," the explanation was repeated.

Isabel stiffened. "May I look at the dolls?"

"Of course. Amber, would you please show Mr. and Mrs. Willoughby our dolls," the headmistress instructed one of the student teachers.

Spaced equally apart, as if in a police lineup, were four different dolls: one white, one black, and one was male . . . looking decidedly gay. The fourth doll had crutches sewn onto its arms, presumably to indicate its irreversible physical impairment.

"I don't care how many strings Larry had to pull, I want our son out of that hothouse of false liberalism immediately," insisted Isabel as they walked toward the valet parkers. "I'll stay on here until Monday so we can look at other schools."

"A black lesbian paraplegic doll would have been a more efficient solution," suggested James in one of his rare displays of practical thinking.

The following Monday, Isabel and James looked at several schools. The first was a "magnet" public school for gifted children. Its playground view was a grid of crackling power lines that threw off enough radiation to shower the children with leukemia.

There was the progressive school in Santa Monica where the

students sat in a semicircle on the floor. During the lesson, they talked with their mouths full of vegan snacks eaten from biodegradable brown bags. When Isabel asked about the program, she was told that there was no program. "Our children learn to love to learn . . . and to recycle," explained the principal.

The School for Early Learning campus was designed by a world-famous architect. Its classrooms featured a one-way mirror for the benefit of goal-oriented parents who insisted on progress they could see for themselves. "The School for Early Materialism" is what Isabel dubbed it after she heard that one of the students brought his mother's ten-carat diamond ring for show-and-tell on "mineral day."

The quota-driven UCLA lab school rescinded Burgo's acceptance after discovering James had checked the square on its application indicating "minority."

"How could you possibly represent our son as a 'minority'?" asked Isabel.

"Burgo is a child from a still-married, heterosexual, social-registered couple. Not only is he in a minority, he can probably qualify as an endangered species," insisted James.

In the end, Isabel and James decided that the only sensible option L.A. offered Burgo in his schooling came from foreigners. Burgo was pulled from the exclusive Beverly Hills school and given over to the French. Le Lycée Français de Los Angeles campus was the old Clara Bow mansion on Overland Drive. The boys wore gray flannel shorts and a tie every day. Grades were posted weekly for all to see. Chairs and desks were lined up in military precision. Everything, including math exercises, was written in blue fountain pen.

"Well, that's just great. . . . French is a dead language, and manners in L.A. are considered a sign of weakness," insisted Monina. "He'll be hooked on Gauloise by the fifth grade."

Despite Monina's warning, it was the right decision . . . the one that made the most sense, given Burgo's parents. Both James and Isabel had the self-imposed confidence of outsiders. Burgo was cut from the same bolt of quirky cloth. They were a nomadic tribe of three, far more comfortable camping with the gypsies on the outskirts of town than settling down with the natives.

38

Almost everything in America eventually becomes entertainment.

James finished his screenplay six months after arriving in L.A. Isabel read it on the plane to New York. It told of a theatrical actor who was having an affair with the older leading lady. The young man was clearly fashioned after James as a younger man; the older actress was transparently Isabel. It was brilliantly written in parts. In whole, it was undeveloped and puerile. What James hadn't fictionalized in his screenplay were the intimate details of his love life with Isabel. It was a disturbing disregard for the most private aspect of their private life together.

Isabel phoned James from the office the next morning.

"It has the beginnings of something interesting, James, but it needs work."

"Just how much work do you think it needs?" asked James. He sounded disappointed.

"I think you need to develop the story . . . it's unrealized."

James didn't respond.

"It's a solid first draft," encouraged Isabel. "I'll give you my notes . . ."

"How lucky I am to have you," said James, sounding slightly less despondent.

"Listen, James, I need to ask something . . ."

"Anything, my dear."

"It's hard not to notice your hero is a twenty-five-year-old version of you, and the older actress is obviously me . . . ironic, given our actual age differences."

"So?"

"So, I've reminded myself it's fiction, and I don't have a problem with how you've cast the characters . . ."

"But?"

"But I can't honestly say I'm not upset that you've described our own lovemaking."

"Oh, Isabel, don't be such a prig."

"I'm not a prig. It would make anyone uncomfortable."

"A writer's life is his material. And besides, who do you think will know other than us?"

"That shouldn't make a difference. What we do in the bedroom belongs between the two of us. I don't want it commercialized."

"I think you're being ridiculously narrow. I would have thought you'd be flattered."

James's lack of inhibition in sharing what Isabel insisted remain private didn't remain an issue long. His script failed to interest anyone. Unreturned phone calls — the death knell to a career in the movie industry — brought an end to James's L.A. odyssey. James fell off the wagon. This time, Isabel was adamant he climb back on. James pulled himself together. They made plans for a permanent return to New York.

"Let's at least change apartments," suggested James.

James's idea of moving from one New York apartment to another first struck Isabel as impractical. A fresh start might do all of us good, was her second thought.

Isabel found a prewar rental near the New York lycée that Burgo would attend in the fall. Determined that her own dislocation would not interfere with family, she continued commuting to the West Coast through the school year. One of her greatest treats was the thirty precious, uninterrupted minutes spent driving Burgo to his school on Friday mornings. During one such car trip, Burgo admitted he was embarrassed to be in the upcoming holiday pageant.

"Do you mean nervous from stage fright?" Isabel asked.

"No, I mean embarrassed," Burgo repeated.

"Why?"

"Because there is no Santa Claus, and he's part of the pageant."

Isabel was crestfallen. She'd made such a point of the holiday celebration. A porcelain pickle was hidden in the branches of their Christmas tree, ensuring luck in the upcoming year, according to German lore. Christmas dinner included a traditional *bûche de Noël* and an English candy peppermint pig. The candy pig came in its own velvet pouch, along with a tiny hammer. It would be passed from one guest to the other after Christmas supper. When the last had his turn at taking a whack, the pieces would be divided — a prelude to prosperity. Isabel loved the idea of Christmas. Nothing — not even her son's disbelief in Santa Claus — would interfere.

"Don't you think the others should know? They'll feel stupid when they find out," suggested Burgo.

"How do *you* know there's no Santa Claus?" Isabel's question was barbed with accusation.

Burgo held fast. "I know," he said.

"What makes you think you're right?" asked Isabel.

"Mommy, how many children are there in the world?"

Isabel realized she was being set up. *He'll be citing centrifugal force and payload next.*

"I have no idea," she replied tartly.

"Just estimate," said Burgo.

"Okay, I'd say about two billion."

Burgo had already done the numbers. "Santa doesn't handle children who aren't Christian . . . that reduces his workload about 15 percent."

Isabel understood where the conversation was going. She was traveling down a narrow one-way street in the wrong direction. Nothing she could say would divert the force of Burgo's logic barreling straight at her.

"So let's give Santa about thirty hours of Christmas to work with," continued Burgo in studious calculation.

Isabel was hoping she might have identified a weak link in her son's argument.

"Why thirty?"

"He'd be crossing the dateline." Burgo paused before asking, "Mommy, what do you think the dateline looks like?"

Isabel had no intention of visualizing the dateline for Burgo's benefit. She was too irked at his unwillingness to allow her Santa Claus.

The car idled in traffic.

"It's impossible. Even with flying reindeer," Burgo said. "Admit it, Mommy, Santa Claus is fiction."

"What about the symbol of a fictional Santa Claus?" Isabel asked, trying her best to regroup and salvage whatever was left of her adult authority.

"What about it?" Burgo asked.

"It represents hope and generosity . . . those are admirable qualities that should be celebrated. Can you think of fictional icons as symbols of something real?"

Finally, Burgo decided to give his mother a graceful way out. "Yes, I can think of other examples."

"They are?"

"Well, Batman is fiction. Ulysses might have been real, but the Cyclops wasn't."

"The waiter in the Greek coffee shop near my office has a kind of Cyclops unibrow," said Isabel. She realized she was digressing when she saw her son's impatient look. "I believe Ulysses was real. Ten years and countless hardships later, he was still trying to return to his wife. Women like to put men to the test, my dear. When your time comes — and it will, Burgo — try to do the right thing."

Burgo ignored his mother altogether.

"Even in our own family, there is fiction and fact," he pointed out resolutely.

"Really?" asked Isabel.

"Yes . . . you are fact; and Papi is fiction," Burgo explained.

After Burgo completed his school year, the Willoughbys moved back to New York. James was grateful to leave behind his failed screenplay and to return to a city where he wasn't the only man wearing a tie. Isabel was no longer required to commute to her family on the weekends. For that she was thankful. James concentrated on his magazine assignments. For that she was relieved. But at the very point James assumed some degree of responsibility in earning an income, he spent it with astonishing abandon.

Money in a marriage measures more than financial progress or social advancement. It gauges that which one spouse expects of the other. James loved his son. He was married happily and faithfully to his wife. But financial obligation was a vagary to him. Far more real was the rush James felt when he placed a bet on the horses, or acted on a risky stock tip, or raised his paddle at auction.

Some part of Isabel recognized this. Some part of her realized that James never really wanted the obligation of loving her. He'll change because there are things in life worth changing for, Isabel had told herself when she had first fallen in love with James. Now, ten years later, when Isabel had no choice but to acknowledge the inaccuracies of that optimistic reassurance, she still wanted to believe it would become true.

3

Isabel traveled the world before recalling the facts. . . .
Learning the truth was another story.

39

There were only two other children in the new apartment building, and they happened to live across from one another on the fourth floor. The unexpected appearance of Burgo — a third child when before there were two — was a formula from the beginning for someone's hurt feelings.

So it was with Billy Tod, the youngest of the three, after he was left out of a heated game of cards. Rejection put him in such a state that he fled in tears. Temporarily forgetting he lived on the fourth floor, Billy appeared crying at the equivalent apartment on the sixth.

Even in a small apartment building, it's not unusual in New York to go for years without knowing your neighbors. Isabel met Billy's attractive and high-strung mother, but had yet to catch sight of his father, who Billy boasted to be the head of the anesthesiology department at New York-Cornell. When Isabel phoned to make sure Billy made it back home after his floor disorientation, his father answered.

"Hello, Dr. Tod, this is Isabel Willoughby, Burgo's mother."

"I was wondering if you'd have the decency to phone."

Isabel would readily admit to a variety of weaknesses — but indecency was not among them. Billy's father was rude and wrong. Isabel had been within earshot of the card game. The other two boys merely suggested Billy sit out a particular game, which accommodated only two players. It drove him to tears. The obvious facts were: Billy's reaction was disproportionate to the circumstances; his crying was prissy for a boy; and, getting lost in such a small building was not high praise for, at the least, his fundamental sense of direction, and at the most, his intelligence. Isabel's first instinct in defense of her son might have been to convey these facts to Billy's father, but she restrained herself. It was, after all, a small building and they'd just moved in. Isabel's reason muscled ahead of her indignation, which had been the first in line for Dr. Tod.

"I'm very sorry — ," Isabel offered before being cut off.

"Billy was extremely upset," Dr. Tod interrupted.

Isabel held her tongue until Dr. Tod was done with his diatribe.

"James," Isabel called, after hanging up the phone, "you won't believe the conversation I just had with Billy's father. I'm hoping a bad day has temporarily put him out of sorts, and it's not something more permanent . . . like his personality."

Come to think of it, Tod means "death" in German, realized Isabel. She called for James again.

"James, there might be a kind of Ingmar Bergman thing going on in Four-A."

James appeared from the next room. Isabel described her unpleasant exchange with their new neighbor. There was a glint in James's eyes as he listened.

"You know, I think we'd be doing an injustice to little Billy if we didn't toughen him up a bit . . . for his own sake," James suggested. "After all, life won't always be sieved by the doorman. I say the next time he visits, we lure him into Central Park with the promise of the zoo; and, in a kind of urban reenactment of the Donner expedition, we abandon him somewhere on the wooded

North End. I wager Billy won't make it back alive, but it's bound to improve his sense of direction if he does."

The following day was Saturday. Isabel and Burgo saw Billy sitting on a bench in front of the bagel store waiting for his father to come out with breakfast. Burgo was just about to apologize for the previous night when a disturbingly short man appeared at Billy's side.

"Daddy, this is Burgo and his mother," said Billy, who stood several inches taller than his father.

If they had a voice, Isabel's eyes would be saying, We don't care how rude it is to stare.

"Billy, would you like to play this afternoon?" Burgo asked. "It would be just you and me."

"What a good idea," said Isabel, relieved that Burgo had taken the lead.

Billy was delighted by the invitation, but Dr. Tod felt compelled to repeat his lecture from the night before. This time it was directed at Burgo.

"Burgo, you're at least one year older than Billy. One year represents a dramatic difference in the rate of development at your age. I hope you understand how upsetting it was for Billy to have been reminded of that last night when you excluded him from your game."

Burgo looked at his mother and saw her begin to coil like a cobra. Before she could strike, he quickly interjected, "I'm sure we'll have a good time when there's just the two of us. . . . Mommy, can Billy come after lunch?"

"Of course. Billy, we look forward to seeing you."

Isabel and Burgo returned to the apartment after their chores. James was getting dressed. Isabel called out from the kitchen as she put the groceries away.

"James . . . we ran into Billy and his father on the street. Darling, can you hear me? You'll never guess . . . James, are you there?"

Just then, the doorbell rang. On his way to answering it, James called back, "I didn't hear a word you said . . . just a minute."

James opened the door.

"How do you do, Mr. Willoughby. I'm Billy's father."

Burgo was reading instructions for his abacus, purchased that morning at the Asia Society's gift store. Isabel was still in the kitchen unpacking groceries. Curiosity got the better of both of them when they heard Dr. Tod's voice.

James was an angularly tall man, almost six and a half feet. Isabel was well over five-ten, and extremely narrow. Not without reason, they produced an attenuated child. Burgo, James, and Isabel were now standing in their apartment's vestibule — like a grouping of Giacometti figures — surrounding Dr. Tod. The scene took on a threatening incongruity.

"Let's all sit down, shall we?" Isabel suggested.

In a professionally flat tone, Dr. Tod explained that it was intellectually confusing — and possibly emotionally damaging — for his son to fraternize with Burgo. It would undermine Billy's self-confidence. While James was processing the absurdity seated on his couch, Isabel quickly agreed. "Whatever you think is best," she said.

Dr. Tod was shown out. Isabel and James suggested to Burgo that he go back to his abacus. They withdrew to the bedroom. Isabel shut the door behind her.

"There's something about him that's wrong," she said in a hushed but urgent tone.

James looked at her concerned face and began to laugh.

"It's not funny."

"My dear, of course it's funny. It's funny and fascinating and poignant all at the same time . . . but it's not wrong."

"I didn't say *it's* wrong, I said, *he's* wrong . . . possibly."

"And just how is he wrong?"

"He's a bully who manipulates the truth."

"That makes him shrewd, for certain, and cynical . . . possibly . . . but not wrong."

"Don't you see?" asked Isabel.

"How can I not? He's shorter than his ten-year-old son," said James.

"That's not the point."

"Well, if that's not the point, I can't imagine what is."

"The point is that he relishes working the margin granted to him because of it . . . especially when he knows you know that's exactly what he's doing, but you won't call him on it."

James thought for a moment.

"Consider it from his perspective, Izzie. No matter how intelligent he is, no matter how he distinguishes himself professionally, regardless of the attractive wife or the Park Avenue address, the world defines him by his missing inches. It's heartbreaking."

"So you believe he deserves more slack than the rest of us because he's short?" Isabel asked, but prevented James an opportunity to answer by insisting, "I don't think there's anything about him that's heartbreaking. I think he's a bitter man. I think he's dangerously mean. And I think he played us like a violin."

Deciding not to walk into the whirling propellers of Isabel's argument, James sat down on the bed. "We should have lunch at the Met this afternoon," he said, hoping his suggestion might distract Isabel from herself.

Isabel's face softened. "I have an alternative to the Met," she said as she unbuttoned her blouse.

40

The neglected Willoughby estate continued to totter its way toward Chekhovian ruin.

The gardens had gone to weed, and almost everything in the dark house was in some phase of moldering. Isabel thought of James's childhood home as a cheerless place. She tried to put a good face on the fact that James and Burgo would be spending the summer there.

"It's nice for Burgo to know at least one of his grandmothers," Isabel suggested to Monina halfheartedly.

"Your mother-in-law brings to mind Mrs. Medlock. Remember the dreaded Mrs. Medlock in *The Secret Garden?*" asked Monina.

"She reminded Ian of Mrs. Danvers in *Rebecca,*" said Isabel, adding, "either way, she thinks of me as an interloper."

"And what do you think of her?" asked Monina.

"I resent her hold on James, and that he always returns there. It's not where we live."

"Treacherous territory, men and their mothers. I wouldn't wander into that bog," said Monina. "What's James doing with himself these days anyway?" she asked.

"Writing a novel."

"About . . . ?"

"I don't know. He's keeping it to himself."

James wrote through the summer and into the following year. Between chapters, he suffered from extravagant lapses in financial judgment. Isabel decided to take a stand when Shepherd & Derom Galleries, not able to locate James, called her at the office to schedule delivery of the William Mulready painting.

"James, we need to have one of those serious talks between husband and wife."

"What a dramatic lead-in," said James. "Well, let me see, serious talks between husbands and wives fall into three categories: infidelity, money, or children. You're my only mistress, so it can't be infidelity. It can't possibly be Burgo, unless you're just about to tell me he's in a holding cell. That leaves money . . . and I don't have any of it, so that can't be it either."

"It's not the amount of money we have or don't have," suggested Isabel. "It's the way it's being spent."

"My dear, one day I'll be rich," said James, not for the first time.

"How? How is it that one day you'll be rich?" asked Isabel.

"I'll sell out," said James in deadpan. "I'm perfectly willing to . . . it's just that nobody's made me an offer yet. Until then, I think we should enjoy what little money we have."

Isabel was determined to hold on to the gravity of their situation, but she couldn't suppress her grin.

"Well, until we get rich, can we agree on something?" she asked.

"Just name it," said James magnanimously, confident he'd managed to sidestep an obviously emotional issue for Isabel.

"Can we agree that we both contribute three-quarters of our

income to the family? The other quarter can be spent in a way neither can complain about. Is that fair enough?" asked Isabel.

James's smile disappeared. "There won't be anything of interest to buy in that price range," he said.

Isabel laughed. Then she realized James was serious.

"Well, darling, if you want to spend on that level, look for more work that produces more income," she suggested.

"I'm not sure I like the way you're assigning me a flowchart," said James with curdled hostility. He quickly reversed course, "I'm sorry, sweetheart. You're right. I'll try my best."

James meant what he said. He knew Isabel was right . . . in theory, at any rate. But he found it impossible to put principal to practice. Their mail continued to overflow with auction catalogues. James didn't employ outright deception when it came to his spending; instead, he became a master at constructing complicated transactions. Shortly after their talk, Isabel returned home from a business trip to discover that James had sold the just-bought Mulready painting to underwrite his purchase of a large Eastlake occasional table now commandeering their bedroom.

It wasn't that Isabel insisted on a thought-out future with James. While most women would have been made anxious by James's wild streak, Isabel loved him the more for it. But as years passed, and Isabel was expected to pick up the ever-increasing slack between James and what reality required of the marriage, life with him leached away her strength and covered her in a fine layer of chalky fatigue.

It wasn't that Isabel couldn't see what was happening. It was that unremitting, impractical, and romantic love intruded between her eyes and all reason, dispossessing her of common sense and holding in abeyance any words of objection.

It was really very simple. There would be no rest for Isabel until she ceased loving James, and that would never be. Their lovemaking consumed all impediments and led to the only conclusion possible — that despite the impossibilities of James, what they had together was priceless.

Rebecca Gibbs asked Isabel to lunch. After discussing various authors and their manuscripts, she ventured into a more personal topic of conversation.

"James gave me his novel," she said.

It was like floating a verbal weather balloon.

"You must know I can't publish my husband's work," Isabel responded.

"It's not publishable."

"Then what's your point?"

"Have you read it?"

"No."

"It's about a future where men are sterile and women govern the world."

Isabel did everything she could to maintain a composed face.

"Feeling a bit emasculated, is he?" asked Rebecca.

"What do I do?" Isabel asked Monina.

"Don't make an issue about the book. It won't be published, so it doesn't matter."

"How does this end?" asked Isabel.

"Something will happen that will bring resolution."

In the years of marriage to James, Isabel tried willing him into the "something" that resembled reason. Her fierce determination worked against everything that was his nature. Not only had James not cooperated, he remained uninterested in the full consequences of his own fallibility.

Isabel's strident need to control was for the sake of an illusion . . . the illusion that order could be implemented. Monina was right . . . if there were to be change in Isabel's unruly life with James, it would be dictated by fate, not by Isabel.

41

On a Friday evening — long after the edict from Billy's father — Burgo and Stuart, the other boy on the fourth floor, were playing in James's office, a converted maid's room off the kitchen. Billy appeared uninvited, enthusiastic, and insisting he'd been granted permission to join the other two boys.

"I don't want anyone's self-esteem shattered by the end of the evening," instructed James in jest as he reached for his coat. "Nothing but confidence-building activity, please. We want everyone to leave here with the same emotional health with which they arrived."

"And where are you off to?" asked Isabel.

"To no good," teased James. "I'll be back in an hour."

Isabel heard happy sounds from the office as she passed its open door while clearing dinner dishes. She offered the children cookies and milk before suggesting that she would walk the two visiting boys down a flight of stairs. That would be unnecessary, said the boys.

Given the previous experience with Billy, Isabel decided to make sure he made it back to his apartment. Billy's father answered the phone.

"I was just about to call you. I'd like you and your husband to come down immediately."

"My husband isn't here," said Isabel. "What seems to be the matter?"

"'What seems to be the matter' should be discussed in person. I suggest you do so with us now, with or without your husband."

Isabel had no idea what could have possibly occurred among the children, when all she had heard was gleeful sounds.

"Why does he want to talk to you?" asked Burgo.

"I have no idea. Burgo, did anything happen to upset Billy?"

"He lost at a game of cards, that's all."

"I'm sure it's nothing. Remember how Billy's father overreacted after the last visit. Just tell Papi to meet me in their apartment. Will you be all right alone?"

"Yes, don't worry," reassured Burgo.

Isabel knocked on the door. She was ushered into the living room. Billy was sitting on his mother's lap. His head was nestled in her chest, and since he was too big a boy to actually fit on his mother's lap, his feet were resting on the floor.

"Billy, tell Mrs. Willoughby exactly what you told us."

Prompted by his father, Billy proceeded to explain — in a trilling birdlike voice — that he had been sexually assaulted. By Burgo.

Never had Isabel heard such lascivious words spoken by anyone, much less a child. Anything Isabel would say or not say took a secondary position to the sinister lie.

"Billy, surely you know that's not true —"

Dr. Tod cut her off. "Don't accuse my son of lying."

Isabel looked over to Mrs. Tod, whose glazed expression gave nothing back. She turned to Dr. Tod.

"Your son is accusing mine of the most unacceptable behavior. You insisted I come down here to discuss this."

Isabel tried to look at Billy, but his face was still buried in his mother's chest.

"Where was Stuart during this time, Billy . . . the time you say Burgo did this thing to you?" Isabel asked.

"He was in the bathroom," muttered Billy.

It was true that there was a bathroom connected to James's office.

"I walked by the room several times and heard you laughing . . . and you stayed for milk and cookies," said Isabel. "Why didn't you say anything?"

"I don't know. But it happened just the way I said."

When Isabel realized that by remaining in the room, she was lending credence to the inquisition, she stood up to leave.

"I have no intention of hearing anything more of this," she said, barely able to contain her rage. "I can't imagine how Billy — or any nine-year-old — would possess familiarity with such lurid acts, or the verbal tools by which to describe them. . . . His words sound suspiciously rehearsed. What goes on in this household is none of my business. But I warn you, Dr. Tod, I warn you that if I ever hear tonight's falsehoods repeated to anyone, I'll come down on you like God's own fury. Surely you don't want that, Dr. Tod. Surely your position at the hospital is more valuable than the venal pleasure you must be taking right now."

"What was it about?" asked Burgo.

"Nothing. But, Burgo, no more play with Billy, all right?"

"Fine by me. . . . He's a sore loser."

"That's the least of it."

James finally made it home that night. He'd been drinking. When Isabel told him what had happened, one part of James admitted he'd left his wife to fend for herself; the other part insisted there was no way he could have known that.

For the first time in the marriage, Isabel denied James their bed.

The next morning James was gone. Tucked under a vase of brightly colored peonies on the kitchen table was a note.

> Ma chère Isabel,
>
> No doubt you are trying to imagine whether you should or can or must bear me. I will try my best to stop dodging what I know will be difficult admissions if you will try to forgive me. You must discover if there is anywhere you do trust me, or you will do nothing but mistrust me.
>
> The truth is, I don't want to lose you. I imagine a Grand Alliance between us, a better form of our pairing . . . we certainly decorate, not to mention other activities, in a brilliantly complementary way. The unforgiving Isabel is a hanging judge. Your counterpart is a clever sneak. I'd like nothing better than to see an end to these villains.
>
> My utmost priority henceforth is you and Burgo. I will do everything and anything, including selling the Willoughby land, to secure Burgo's future and earn you some well-deserved security. I want to try to support us. There's only one place that will allow us to live on a single income, where Burgo will be well educated without the cost of tuition, where we can't help but be happy. Come to Paris and let me take care of you. It's what we both need.

Trusting everything written in James's letter — with no other purpose but to stay married to the man she still loved — Isabel resigned from her job and moved the family to Paris.

42

The croupier was now James . . . he was the one redealing the deck of cards and handling the chips.

James became the Paris correspondent for several American magazines; his pay — along with the rent for subleasing their New York apartment — would support the family while they lived in Paris. The year was a gift from James to Isabel . . . hers to do as she wanted. Only once they settled — and only if she wished — would she edit a small number of manuscripts on a freelance basis.

Isabel filled out the reams of paperwork required by the French Consulate for a *carte de séjour* and packed up in New York. James went ahead to locate a Paris apartment and enroll Burgo in sixth grade at the lycée.

France is a country where the government pays its citizens' way through school; where statesmen are often scholars; where everyone, no matter their class, has a love affair with food and beauty. The history of Paris is the history of all France.

Paris in the nineteenth century was gripped by despair and lawlessness before Napoleon III realized that in order to keep fractious mobs from blockading the narrow streets, he needed to change the very layout of the city. His *préfet de la Seine,* Baron

Georges-Eugène Hausmann, a Paris-born German descendant, was charged with that near-impossible task. Hausmann's German genes — not his French birth — enabled him to unsentimentally raze large sections of the city, eliminate entire neighborhoods, and demolish hundreds of buildings . . . all for the sake of order. He systematized Paris into twenty distinct parts — arrondissements — which start to count "one" at the city's nucleus, the Louvre, and spiral out clockwise to the twentieth. Each has its own distinct character and style.

The sixteenth arrondissement is a quietly bourgeois, largely residential corner of Paris bordered by the Bois de Boulogne. It happens to have an excellent public school. James concentrated on a small section of the sixteenth called Auteuil. Auteuil features elegant buildings and a quaint town square where its long, elegant streets converge, channeling well-disposed, elegant people. James had managed to find an exquisite two-bedroom apartment in a limestone *hôtel particulier.* It was piped by a black wrought-iron balcony and offered a leafy view of the Bois.

Burgo's school was only two blocks away. Its view was the Jardin des Serres, where cathedral-height greenhouses had originally been part of Louis XV's botanical gardens. Isabel and Burgo walked to his school through a market that opened before dawn. True to unwelcoming Parisian form, no other parent would speak to Isabel, even though her child was greeted by theirs with a handshake and *Ca va?*

The school's concierge lived in a small ground-floor apartment off the vestibule. At 8:00 A.M. exactly and without fail, the building's enormous wood door would rattle from the inside. It would open just wide enough for her decrepit, watery-eyed dog — emitting wheezing sounds from one end, and gas from the other — to waddle out among the children. Madam concierge appeared right behind her dog. With the air of someone very much in charge of crucial information, she would post the day's lunch menu, dictated by ingredients the school's cook had chosen from the open-air market earlier that morning.

The school fed the children according to seasonal fruits and vegetables; there was always fresh fish or meat, a salad and cheese course, and a sweet. Uneaten bread from lunch was later toasted and offered with jam at three o'clock as the children's *goûté*. At the beginning of the school year, Isabel and James were asked whether they wished to be billed for Burgo's meals. When the first invoice arrived, they thought there was a digit missing. No, they were told, the bill was correct. It was the equivalent of a few dollars a week.

Every morning, Isabel watched Burgo disappear into the school's front vestibule . . . a tall, rangy boy in a single line of small, narrow-hipped French children. On her way back to the apartment she would happily lose herself in the dense cluster of the market's kiosks. Isabel wandered among the stalls of cheeses, teas, jams, and just-slaughtered ducks with iridescent necks. One counter featured nothing but potatoes, each variety in its own box, meticulously labeled in neat, cursive handwriting. Another displayed different kinds of mushrooms: some smooth as white round buttons, others smelling of ancient earth, knarred like witches' fingers.

Isabel would spend hours in the market selecting just the right tomato or discovering a new cheese. Returning home whenever the spirit moved her, Isabel would unpack her delicacies, read *Le Figaro,* edit whatever manuscript she was working on, and lunch with James on the treasures found in the market. They would make unhurried love, nap, and take a late-afternoon espresso among the architectural swirls of a café designed by Guimard on the nearby rue de la Fontaine.

Isabel would meet Burgo in front of his school in the early

evening. He would shake hands with his schoolmates and bid them *á demain* before kissing his mother on both cheeks hello. Stopping at the boulangerie for the dinner baguette, Burgo would rip off the warm tip of the loaf's tail and eat it on the way home. Parisians walking home in all twenty of the city's arrondissements were enjoying that same simple pleasure.

Clichés about the French are laughably accurate: they are rarefied and pretentious people. But it seems they are also willing to dress up as vegetables in order to appear on quiz shows.

After dinner — armed with the excuse of improving their French — James, Isabel, and Burgo would watch TV game shows. Thirty minutes of witnessing how ridiculous the French could actually be, given the opportunity, provided just the right degree of perspective before Burgo settled down to exceedingly serious homework — homework that called on him to memorize, and then recite for biology class, a two-page, single-spaced list of all personal physicians to the French kings . . . and, for his civics class, gruesome statistics on how many people in Paris are hospitalized for slipping on what their dogs leave behind.

Weekends had their own delightful routine. Saturday afternoons were given over to the American Library, where Burgo read his way through H. G. Wells and Isabel browsed the previous week's Sunday *New York Times.* On the way home, they'd stop at their favorite patisserie on the rue de l'Université. Sunday was earmarked for the Bois: a favorite discovery was the Jardin Shakespeare, featuring specimens of plants and trees mentioned in Shakespeare's plays. Every other Sunday, Burgo took his riding lesson at the Pony Club, linked to the Porte Maillot metro stop by a small, open air train. On a warm day, there was always a trip to Ile Saint-Louis for the sole purpose of Berthillon *glaces.*

★　★　★

James and Isabel marked their twelfth anniversary in Paris. From the beginning of the marriage, they had been each other's intellectual counterweight. They had remained passionate lovers and had become coconspirators in rearing their son. But never had James allowed Isabel to feel entirely safe. James was dangerously unreliable, and Isabel had been very close to buckling under the ever-increasing weight of responsibility. Life in New York had slivered her into sharp, efficient segments.

Isabel in Paris was a different matter. She became a rambling, sensual run-on sentence. Drifting from one sublime day to the next, she found peace she'd never known . . . a safe happiness, like her lazy nap in the hammock the time she and James meandered down the Amazon River on a slow boat.

The dream was wrong, repeated Isabel's happiness to itself. And, as she lulled herself into believing something that wasn't true, the trail of words disappeared, and the path behind it became overgrown.

The Romans called it Lutetia. They hired barbarian mercenaries to defend it.

Empires have been won and lost in Paris. Paris has crowned the heads of kings, and has severed those of aristocrats. For over two millennia, Paris has been a city stained with the blood of invasions, revolts, wars, riots, murderous feuds, and crimes of passion.

Paris is where Isabel tried to kill James.

43

So how did your happiness lead to attempted murder?" asked Dr. Lewis.

It was Isabel's third session with the psychiatrist. She'd managed thus far to preserve her psychological privacy by relaying the facts in a discursive way . . . providing just enough information to keep Dr. Lewis on track, but not enough to allow him any real insight.

Now they were at the crucial point, and Isabel was cupping secrecy in both hands, as if it were a precious liquid she would not let slip through her fingers.

"Go back to the beginning of Paris," said Dr. Lewis.

"Why? I've told you all you need to know about Paris," said Isabel insolently.

"Obviously there's something missing."

"What's missing is the truth."

"Okay, go back to the beginning of the truth," said Dr. Lewis.

"Don't you understand?" she asked.

Isabel's impenetrable facade began to show tiny fissures. "Don't you understand?" she asked again, this time averting her eyes so as not to reveal the vulnerability of having asked at all.

Dr. Lewis didn't answer.

"I don't know how far back I need go to find the truth," she said.

He still didn't respond.

"What if there is no truth to the story?" asked Isabel. Her voice was shaking, and she was perilously close to tears. "What if it's all a writer's invention?"

"Don't rely on the words," said Dr. Lewis. "Try to remember what you did. Did you stay in Paris the entire year?"

"No. I went back to New York. I had to. I was editing a manuscript, and I needed to work with the author in person."

"How long were you gone?"

"About ten days."

"And . . . ?"

"And, while I was in New York, I discovered something . . . something James kept secret."

"What was it?"

"Our accountant told me we owed a great deal more in taxes. I insisted it was her miscalculation because my taxes had been taken directly from my payroll check, and James had already paid his quarterly estimates."

"So?"

"So it turned out that he liquidated his IRA prematurely in order to buy a painting. It was taxed at my bracket . . . to make matters worse, there were penalties."

"You returned to Paris."

"Yes."

"And you confronted him . . ."

"Not right away."

"Why not?"

"He'd bought a dog while I was gone."

"He bought a dog without mentioning it in any of your phone conversations?"

"No."

"Well, I suppose the dog is no more peculiar than anything else you've described about James."

"You're missing the point."

"What point is that?"

"He bought the dog the same way he drinks."

"I thought he stopped drinking."

"I thought so too, until I came back from New York."

"So, while in New York, you were informed you owed more to the IRS because James bought a painting but hadn't told you. You returned to Paris to find he'd bought a dog, and he'd been drinking."

"I knew James bought the dog before I came back."

"How?"

"He relied on Burgo to tell me. Apparently the dog was hanging in the hall."

"I beg your pardon?"

"There was a portrait of a dog in the hallway of James's childhood home. He loved the painting, but it was sold at auction."

"You say the painting was sold at auction?"

"That's right."

"I assume the painting he bought with the IRA money wasn't the dog painting sold when he was a child . . . otherwise there'd be no reason to buy the real dog."

"Good for you, Doctor," Isabel said belligerently. "The painting he bought with the IRA money was a Christen Købke portrait. But as a kind of bonus to what I'm sure are the copious notes you must be transcribing as soon as I leave this office, James later told me he searched for a dog that was a physical replication of the dog in the childhood painting. One that had the same markings. The dog in the painting was called Admiral, and he named the dog he bought Colonel."

"I'm not sure my notes would do this justice," said the doctor.

"You're right," said Isabel. She almost smiled.

"What did you do when you walked into the apartment?" asked Dr. Lewis. "You were glad to be back. You knew you needed to confront James about the taxes. You were greeted by a dog your husband depended on your son to tell you about."

"I did what I always do," said Isabel. "I bit down on my resentment and drew a bath. Burgo was delighted by the dog, which made it more difficult for me to object."

"So the dog turned out to be a nonissue . . ."

"What in God's name is a *nonissue*? . . . What kind of smug word is that?"

"Right now, we're not dealing with words. Did the dog bother you?"

"Not enough to try to kill my husband over it, no." Isabel finally allowed a smile. "Actually, I fell in love with the dog."

"So it wasn't the dog?"

"It was how the dog came to be. James had been studying classified ads in dog magazines to locate a breeder. He rented a car in order to pick up the dog, which was kenneled in the country. It took effort and planning over a period of several weeks. I never knew about it."

"What about the drinking? Was that on the sly as well?"

"Do you really think he'd discuss it with me beforehand?" suggested Isabel sarcastically.

"Then how did you learn about it?"

Isabel flinched. The psychiatrist had hit a nerve.

"Isabel?"

"I heard you."

Isabel wasn't looking at Dr. Lewis. She was gazing through his ground-floor window and into the apartment building's common back garden, where she saw fleeting images of Paris, disparate and haphazard . . . images her mind tried to organize . . . from background to foreground . . .

. . . It was the weekend. Isabel had included Burgo in a surprise. A peace offering of sorts to James about the dog . . . before addressing the more serious issue of their outstanding tax bill. Isabel had measured the dog's neck and custom-ordered a black collar with "Colonel" engraved on its silver name plaque.

"It's terribly expensive, but the dog is obviously dear to Papi," said Isabel as they walked past the scarves to the back of Hermès, where the saddles were displayed.

"If you consider the cost of the collar over Colonel's lifetime, it actually works out to be quite reasonable," suggested Burgo, who almost always saw life from a mathematical point of view.

"You're absolutely right. Now that you've put it in the proper perspective, Burgo, I can afford to treat us to Ladurée afterwards."

Isabel and Burgo polished off a plate of *marrons* before heading to the American Library. As they emerged from the Trocadero metro stop, words changed Isabel's life in a way that couldn't be stopped.

"Did you know there's a bistro in this neighborhood that serves over a hundred kinds of red wine, all by the glass?" Burgo asked, trying to sound casual.

The cold stone of anger lodged in Isabel's middle and then moved up to her throat. It was one thing for Burgo to stand in for James with the news of a dog; another thing entirely for him to become the keeper of his father's secrets. Burgo had carefully selected the words to tell his mother what needed to be told without losing what bound him to silence.

Words had been spoken, and they created a force continuum. Never before had Isabel felt such fury. Words had been spoken, and something was bound to happen.

44

"Was it premeditated?"

"No," Isabel answered the psychiatrist. "Lucky for me I tried killing my husband in the one country that allows you to get away with murder. Under the right set of circumstances, the French forgive crimes of passion or provocation . . . the discovery of a lover or mistress, for instance."

"And you . . . what provoked you?"

Isabel struggled to visualize a single side of the origami she'd carefully constructed to fold around the truth.

It had been raining that day.

Only after Isabel remembered the rain was she able to remember the rest. . . .

"After our stop at the American Library, Burgo and I went home. By the time we arrived, it was beginning to drizzle. I asked James to take a walk with me. . . . I told him there was something we needed to talk about. I took an umbrella. But by the time we stepped outside, the rain had stopped . . ." Isabel trailed off.

The umbrella was from Madeleine Gely. It was the color of burnt sienna. Its long straight handle narrowed into a pointed silver-tipped end.

"We were walking down boulevard Suchet," said Isabel. "I

told James I knew he was drinking. I told him that I was furious that he'd put our son in an impossible position."

"And how did he respond?"

"With words that sent me out of control . . . ," said Isabel.

"Start at the beginning," said Dr. Lewis.

"We'd just come to the rotary at Porte de St. Cloud. It was rush hour. The French are deliberately reckless drivers . . . cars were cutting each other off . . . hurtling in different directions. Yes, James admitted, he had asked Burgo to keep the drinking between them. He said he then corrected the situation when Burgo insisted it was wrong. He said he told Burgo he could tell me whatever he wanted. He said that Burgo didn't tell me because the drinking wasn't what mattered to Burgo so much as his awareness of how angry it would make me, and how dissension endangered his home. James told me he'd not been dishonest, not in the true sense of the word.

"Dishonesty would have been denying that he'd been drinking, he said. Since, on second thought, he had told Burgo to tell me whatever he wanted about it, his self-serving judgment was convenient . . . a way of continuing a behavior he was enjoying and at the same time avoiding a storm. It was the weirdest admission . . . as though he was talking in the third person about someone other than himself. There were no regrets . . . just James's blind indifference to the injury he'd caused. And then he said I'd done the same at one time . . . that I hadn't told him about 'my people' until the night before we were married.

"He saw me raise the umbrella and assumed I was just about to open it. Of course that would be what I'd do, because it was beginning to rain. But I didn't open the umbrella. I swung it. I swung with all my force. It smashed against the side of his head.

The tip ripped open his scalp. I remember the rain diluting the blood into pink watercolor that dripped off his face. Most of all, I remember his look of disbelief. First disbelief . . . then fear. I was out of control. He'd never seen that before, and it frightened him.

"I *was* out of control, but I was also aware of what I was doing, and I wanted to kill him. I lunged at him with the umbrella and tried stabbing him with it. He grabbed the tip and wrestled the umbrella away from me. I still wanted him dead, but I had no more weapon, so I became the weapon and I shoved him. I shoved him with all my strength into traffic. The pavement was wet, and he slipped.

"It all happened in a flash," said Isabel who now seemed oddly tranquil, "with the kind of adrenaline-pumped strength you read about in the tabloids. The kind where the mother picks up the front of a Mack truck in order to save her baby pinned underneath. I pushed him into the oncoming cars . . . and then I ran. I ran without looking back. Afterward, my voice was hoarse."

It was the only break in the telling of Isabel's story. "I was screaming while I was hitting him. What was I screaming?" she asked herself.

Then it came to her . . .

"I remember now," she said.

Isabel looked at Dr. Lewis.

"I remember now . . . I was screaming, 'Look what you've done!'"

There was a momentary pause.

"That wasn't the end, was it?" asked the doctor.

"No, that wasn't the end. There was more. There was always more to James. He was like an impossible test of endurance."

"What happened afterward?"

"I wandered around in a daze until I remembered Burgo was

home alone. By the time I managed to find my way back to the apartment, my clothes were soaked through and my hair was dripping. I didn't want anyone to see me, so I took the stairs instead of the lift."

Isabel's attention drifted.

"And . . . ?" asked Dr. Lewis. "What happened next? You took the steps . . . and?"

Isabel's eyes met his.

"What happened on the steps, Isabel?"

"I walked up the stairs to the small landing between the second and third floor. James was on the next landing. He couldn't make the last flight of steps. He was slouching against the wall, bloodied and drenched . . . his scalp was ripped open, and his clothes were torn."

"Were you relieved to see him alive?"

"I'm not sure. I climbed the flight of stairs between us, and without either of us saying a word . . ."

"What?" asked Dr. Lewis.

No answer.

"Isabel, what happened in the hallway?"

"We had sex against the wall."

The doctor didn't react.

"Do you think me insane?" asked Isabel

"It's extreme behavior, but not insane," said Dr. Lewis. "Passion thrives on danger and impossibility. You wanted to kill your husband in the one vicious moment you had no choice but to take him at his word. It's easy to point to drinking as what you believe to be his failings. . . . It gives you the moral high ground. Drinking or no, James never played by the rules. . . . What made you think he would for you or Burgo?"

"Hope," whispered Isabel.

"I'm sorry, I didn't hear you."

"I didn't stop."

"Stop what?"

"Hoping."

"No. I gather not. I gather you continued living together until something else happened. Tell me what could possibly be more compelling a reason to leave a marriage than an attempted murder."

"Betrayal," said Isabel.

"Why is that . . . why do you think that?" asked Dr. Lewis.

Isabel stared at Dr. Lewis with a grieved look that spoke of finality before words did.

"Because betrayal kills hope."

45

It was June when her father phoned Isabel in Paris with the news her mother had died.

"How?" asked Isabel.

"An aneurism," said her father.

"Were you there?"

"No."

"Was anyone?"

"No."

"In all these years, did she ever say anything about me?"

Rufus didn't answer.

"Nothing? Nothing at all?"

"I'm sorry, Isabel."

"Where will she be buried?"

"According to her will, her remains are to be sent to a funeral home in Budapest."

"Budapest? I thought whatever family she had was buried in Vienna?"

"I did too, but she left instructions . . . she wants her ashes scattered in the Danube, of all the damn things."

"Who'll take care of it?" asked Isabel.

"The funeral director, I would guess," said her father.

"Don't you think one of us should go?"

"Your mother's instructions were that no one attend. I'm making arrangements for a service here," said Rufus who was determined to have the last word on the woman he loved . . . even though he knew that she, possibly, had loved no one.

The month before her mother died, Isabel accepted a job in New York to run the literary division of a big talent agency. Since the incident, neither James nor Isabel had mentioned her failed attempt to kill him. After their sexual encounter in the hallway, they went to the American Hospital, where James took forty-two stitches in his scalp. Burgo was told James had slipped on the wet pavement into the street and was hit by a car. Much the way Burgo's French history book avoided any reference to the Vichy government, whatever occurred between James and Isabel that day simply hadn't happened.

Isabel's new job would start in September, which coincided with Burgo's enrollment at the lycée in New York and a sizable rent hike for the apartment there. Isabel decided that, rather than returning to Paris after her mother's service, it would make more sense to go directly to New York and look for another apartment.

As Isabel's chances with James continued to diminish, her attentions began to unconsciously drift toward the other male in the family . . . the one who offered a world still full of possibilities. Isabel was grateful for Burgo, because she was only able to come to each new beginning with James with whatever strength was left from the countless other beginnings.

They had always been renters . . . renters of apartments, of houses, of cars. After so many relocations, Isabel thought ownership might anchor James to something other than the Willoughby estate. She found what she thought to be a charming apartment within walking distance to the lycée and the Met. The man, his dog, and the boy will be happy, thought Isabel. Working against every one of her fiscally conservative inclinations, Isabel took out a large mortgage to purchase the apartment.

The family would reunite after school let out. That was the plan. James would make a quick trip to New York after supervising Burgo and Colonel's transport from Paris to his mother in Virginia. He would spend the summer in Virginia. Isabel would join them there in late August after she unpacked what had been moved from Paris.

Everything was put in order and in place. But instead of feeling a sense of permanence, Isabel felt unease.

The dream had emerged from seclusion. The dream of James leaving. It filtered through the jagged dark of her sleepless nights.

While Isabel was in New York, struggling to come to terms with her marriage, James was in Paris having a mental debate on the same subject.

What exactly does she want from me? began his interior monologue. Nothing had been wrong, he thought; but for the last few years, it didn't seem Isabel could find anything right. And recently, even the most casual conversation with her required a battle plan.

Bloody hell . . . she tried to kill me. Actually, thought James to himself, her murder attempt made Isabel even more bewitching.

She knows how I feel about her. James had just written a magazine article, which included an admiring reference to Isabel and his marriage. Isabel hadn't seen it yet, but James felt confident that she'd be impressed when she did.

It's the drink, he admitted begrudgingly. Well, too goddamn

bad. James always felt better if a drink was within sight. It didn't make him less of a good husband . . .

The spending, that annoys her too, grumbled James. She'd confronted him over the Købke painting and his IRA money. Why shouldn't I bring beautiful things into our lives? James wondered.

The more James thought about it, the more put off he was by Isabel's expectations. The more James reflected, the more he resented Isabel's demands.

Life had become a series of negotiations between what he wanted and what Isabel insisted was reasonable. James wondered what it would be like to return to New York.

Isabel had signed a lucrative employment contract. What about me? James asked himself. Where am I in this? James's income hadn't increased, and he was in his late fifties. New York would require a certain level of earning from James. So would Isabel, if he intended to enjoy himself.

James considered all of these issues after just having returned from the Drouot and what had been his second look at the most beautiful Pugin sideboard. He was punching the key code to the apartment building's front door when the postman arrived and handed him Isabel's letter.

Dear J,

I love you immeasurably. But I don't think I can keep up any longer. It's completely depleted me . . . emotionally, physically, financially. If we're to continue together, it has to be a different way . . . without the drink and the spending. I must tell you now, James, I have only enough left for one more new start.

There had been a single instant that was the beginning of James and Isabel . . . a moment that could be isolated from all the other moments in their lives. Isabel was able to recall it precisely. It occurred the night of their dinner at À Sousceyrac. She was coming down the shallow bank of stairs outside the Hotel Saint-Simon at the same time James was coming around the car to open her door. That was the moment that marked the beginning of them.

There was no such precision to the end of James and Isabel. It was foreshadowed in Isabel's letter, to be sure. At the time she wrote the letter, she knew it was no longer possible to continue the life they had, but Isabel didn't have the slightest doubt James would change. Hope convinced her of that. After all was said . . . all the pretty words pirouetting around them . . . what was most important was what would be done. The marriage was at stake. James would know in the most visceral way — in a way that had nothing to do with words — that in order to stay married to Isabel, things had to change. *He will act in a way that will make our lives together possible.* That was Isabel's hope.

James might have acted . . . just as Isabel had hoped. But something else showed up. Something easier. Something that protected him from decision. Something that released him from obligation. Something James had been waiting for all of his life.

Money.

Money is what showed up. So much of it, even James couldn't have imagined. So much money that James's moral sense was lost between the ends and means of its vast expanse.

46

It was all in the timing.

The fates sent The Money to James in Paris the day after he received Isabel's letter. At the time The Money unexpectedly and
conveniently dropped in his lap, James understood he wouldn't
get another chance at it. Not at this level.

And so, in the most hardened, matter-of-fact way for a man
who was such a romantic — employing the most deliberate tac-
tics for a man who was known to be notoriously vague; revealing
the most ignoble intentions for a man who thought of himself as
slightly more noble than others — James decided to choose The
Money. James chose it over everything else in his life.

The Money took effect on James almost immediately. It
eliminated hindrance. It ignored inconvenience. It overrode objection. It empowered. James didn't bother to wait until Isabel's
back was turned . . . he deceived in front of her. With a sanguine
perspective endowed by the most expensive suite in the Plaza
Athénée, *Nothing can touch me* was the self-declaration blocking
any concern that someone during some part of his covert weekend in New York might mention to Isabel that they had seen him.

On Saturday afternoon, while she was jockeying for a better
view of the roasted artichokes behind the glass counter at E.A.T.,

someone did mention it. An acquaintance bumped into Isabel in the takeout queue.

"Isabel, I'd heard you'd returned to New York. How are you?" he inquired. "And what a surprise to see James in a rowboat . . . he's really thrown himself back into the city."

"I can't imagine what you're talking about," said Isabel.

"This morning, in the park —"

"James is still in Virginia with Burgo. He's due tomorrow."

"How odd. I was rowing with my son in Central Park this morning, and I was sure I saw James in another boat."

"Well, he's not in town."

"I could have sworn it was James."

"He's not here . . . and even if he were, do you really think James would be in a rowboat?" asked Isabel.

"You're right, it would be seriously out–of–character. . . . There was another person in the boat. A woman in a full-length fur coat. Actually, that's what caught my eye."

"In from Palm Beach for the weekend," said Isabel ruefully.

"Did you just land?" Isabel asked James when he phoned Monday morning on his way into the city.

"I'm coming in from the airport," was his answer . . . true in the literal sense, since he was, in fact, coming from the airport. But at the time he was calling his current wife, James was being driven back into the city by a chauffeur employed by his future wife who had just waved good-bye from the door of her private plane. She was flying to San Francisco where she'd visit friends while James left Isabel. Once Isabel was told she was being left, the plane would return to New York to extricate James from what was certain to be awkward circumstances . . . and whisk him away from any accountability.

Isabel had absolutely no idea.

Despite her cosmopolitan sophistication, despite her acute intelligence, despite her refined sensibility, despite everything about Isabel, she was a perfect fool.

And James? What of James? If asked to justify himself, James would say he simply allowed Isabel to believe what she wanted . . . yes, it might have been the omission of truth; but, no, it wasn't a lie.

It wasn't a lie. Somehow, it was worse. By manipulating Isabel's implicit trust in him, James was able to deftly circumvent the explicit truth. How he managed it was staggeringly cold-blooded. . . .

Just as he said he would, James traveled to the Willoughby place from Paris. As planned, he spent a few days settling Burgo and Colonel with his mother before his trip to New York where Isabel was waiting. But instead of arriving in New York on Monday morning, as he had agreed with Isabel, James arrived two days before — unbeknownst to her — with the woman to whom he had become engaged.

It has been said that hypocrisy is the tribute that vice pays to virtue.

James stood when Isabel entered the room; and James pulled out her chair when they had lunch during what she assumed was his first day back in New York. James walked on Isabel's outside as they strolled up Madison Avenue afterward. James continued to display the amenities of respect toward Isabel; and all the while, James was engaged to another woman. In fact, James had been engaged for five of the six weeks between receiving Isabel's letter and coming through the front door of the recently purchased New York apartment.

James spent Monday night with Isabel. It seemed to her that he liked the new apartment, but the next morning he unexpectedly announced he wanted to return to Virginia that afternoon. He said he didn't want Burgo to feel left behind after having so recently reentered the States. Isabel was disappointed their conjugal visit was cut short, but understood James's paternal concern. She had a lunch with a friend she couldn't cancel on such short notice. James promised he'd phone from Virginia. Isabel kissed him good-bye after saying, "I'll get there as soon as I can. Take care of our boy."

James decided he need not choose words to tell Isabel he'd already left her. He used another way. One that risked no misunderstanding. Isabel returned to the apartment after lunch, and resting on top of the unopened mail were photographs. James left photographs . . . but only after James himself left. He left without saying a word. Not one awkward, unhappy word.

The photographs James intended Isabel to find were devoid of the slippery properties of innuendo. What was said was nakedly obvious. How was it possible that Isabel didn't accept what anyone — everyone — would have seen?

It had to do with what Isabel expected of intellect. The woman in the photographs appeared wholly without spirit, and, by implication, charm. Certainly not the mind, thought Isabel.

It had to do with what Isabel expected of intimacy. There was no visible spark between James and the woman — they were standing together, side by side, but nothing appeared to be connecting them. Certainly not sex, thought Isabel.

It had to do with taste. In the rowboat photograph, the woman looked overpowered by her out-of-season Fendi fur. In the photo of them in the country, her stiffly coiffed hair resembled a helmet; she wore a matronly outfit accessorized with a gladiator brooch. Style that scarcely fires one's imagination, thought Isabel.

Had Isabel been more worldly, she might have surmised that something else was going on that didn't have to do with sex, intellect, or style. Isabel might have considered that the woman — lacking everything that would otherwise interest James — was secondary to the one and only thing that distinguished her . . . her money.

A heavy, thick, velour curtain of denial unfurled from the rafters, and Isabel was unable to see what James had so obviously staged.

She put the photographs away, and turned her attention to the blinking light on the answering machine. There were two messages, both for James. One was from Lobb — the English boot maker — informing him that his shoes were ready. Isabel thought it extremely odd, because James hadn't been in London, and it took Lobb at least two months to make shoes. A better point was that James had nowhere near the financial wherewithal for such a purchase. The other phone message was from a dealer in Paris, trying to verify James's Virginia address before shipping the Pugin sideboard. Isabel froze. Pugin required more than was housed in their combined savings.

She phoned JP Morgan's twenty-four-hour customer service. No withdrawals had been made from their joint account. Where had he found the money? wondered Isabel.

47

"What do you mean, he's not there?"

Isabel was jolted from angst to panic when she was told by his mother that James hadn't returned to Virginia.

"Where's Burgo?"

"Burgo is here with me and is just fine," said Mrs. Willoughby. "He spent the day teaching Colonel commands in English."

"I'd like to speak to him after we're done."

"Of course, he's just outside."

"Mrs. Willoughby, where is James? I don't think it unreasonable to expect an answer."

"You started it, Isabel. Surely, at this point, you're not surprised."

"I started what? Exactly what was it that I started?"

"You wrote to James that you wanted a divorce."

Isabel was blindsided. James had shared what should have remained a marital matter with his mother, one he'd obviously misrepresented.

"Am I to understand you know where he is, but aren't willing to tell me?"

"This is between the two of you. I really don't think I should get involved."

"I'd like to speak to Burgo now," said Isabel barely able to finish her sentence.

Isabel kept her violent emotions from Burgo. "Hello, darling, I understand from Grammy that you're giving Colonel a Berlitz course. Is he bilingual yet?" she asked in feigned calm.

"He needs more work," said Burgo.

"Well, get him in line before he arrives in New York . . . there are leash laws here. And how is his trainer?"

"I'm fine, Mommy."

"Burgo, Papi is taking some time to himself . . . but he's coming back soon."

"I know."

"Will you be all right without him for the next few days?"

"I'm fine, Mommy," Burgo said for the second time.

"Okay, then, I'll check in tomorrow. Big kiss good night."

"You too."

Isabel hung up the phone and poured herself a cup of tea. She sat alone in agonizing confusion, refusing to relinquish the belief that James's abandonment was a dreadful misunderstanding. It took a fact-checker to bring Isabel to her senses.

The publishing process of a magazine moves forward in a series of separately executed sprints. Positioned as the third to last runner in a relay race, the fact-checker is called on to perform his task with meticulous attention to detail before passing the baton to the copyeditor, who passes it to a proofreader, who must cross the finish line of the printer's deadline.

James's article — the article he wrote while he was in Paris, but before he received Isabel's letter; the article Isabel had yet to read; the article in which James referred admiringly to Isabel as

the woman responsible for his many years of blissful marriage —
that article had been scheduled for the November issue of *Town &
Country*. With a four-month lead time, the piece was being put to
bed in July. James gave his Virginia number to the fact-checker.
He wasn't there when she called. Only when pressed did Mrs.
Willoughby provide a forwarding phone number. It was for a
hotel in San Francisco, where James had been registered by a
woman, under her own name. The fact-checker assumed it was
Isabel's maiden name. They're on a second honeymoon, reasoned
the fact-checker, which would explain why James's mother was so
reticent in disclosing his whereabouts.

The happenstances were like a long line of upright domi-
noes. After the first piece had been pushed over, it took a surprisingly short time for the last piece to topple.

It happened that Isabel was a good friend of a writer who
also wrote for *Town & Country*. She had an article scheduled for
the same issue, and was on the same deadline as James. It happened the same fact-checker was working simultaneously on both
articles. It happened that the fact-checker had worked previously
with Isabel's friend, but had never worked with James. She knew
Isabel was married to James, but didn't know Isabel's maiden
name. The fact-checker mentioned in her late-night phone conversation with Isabel's friend, Eileen, that James and Isabel were in
San Francisco. But Eileen had just had lunch with Isabel in New
York that same day.

"Isabel, this is Eileen . . ."

"Did I leave something behind?"

"Listen, I've spent the last few hours trying to decide if I
should tell you this. . . ."

"The suspense is worse than whatever you've phoned to say,"
said Isabel.

"I wish that were the case. . . . Oh, God, this is awkward, but I'll just . . . Have you and James separated?"

"Why are you asking?"

"Remember I told you during lunch that I have an upcoming piece in *Town & Country*?"

"Yes . . ."

"Apparently James also has a piece scheduled for the same issue, and the same fact-checker is working on both of our pieces."

"Yes . . ."

"She located him in San Francisco today."

"Who located whom in San Francisco?" asked Isabel.

"The fact-checker was on deadline. She couldn't find James until she tracked him down in San Francisco."

"He's in Vir —" Isabel stopped herself, realizing where the conversation was leading her.

"She assumed you were traveling with him," continued Eileen. "But of course you're not, and I —"

Isabel couldn't stand hearing more. "What you're trying to tell me is that he's in San Francisco with someone else."

"I'm so sorry, Isabel. Do you want to know her name? I have her name."

"What difference would a name make?"

Isabel's hands, shaking uncontrollably, barely managed to put the receiver back in its cradle. Blood stopped flowing to her extremities. Her stomach solidified into a hard core. Her throat tightened, and her mouth went dry. Isabel's physical self switched to automatic pilot and moved her away from the phone, to the kitchen sink for a glass of water, then onto the couch.

Taking shallow breaths, unable to swallow, Isabel held a full glass of water in her lap and heard her brain replay one thought over and over again, as though on a looped tape. That single thought drove Isabel's brain into her soul . . .

James has been with another woman.

Convinced her husband still intended to communicate, Isabel checked her e-mail. There were two, neither from James.

One was from Eileen:

Dear Isabel,

I don't feel right holding on to this information. It goes to the grave with me. Suzie Evans, the Campton Hotel in San Francisco.

The other was from an English friend:

Dearest Isabel,

James was here several weeks ago on his way to Ireland. I told him he was a fool. I'm here if you want to talk.

Yours in admiration and with love,

Annabel

48

There was something sordid about reaching into the recesses of the drawer to bring them into the light.

When she found the photographs that afternoon, Isabel had hastily shoved them to the far back of the drawer before her brain had a chance to process the visual information. She remembered now that a date was digitally printed on the lower left side of each photo.

Isabel spread the photos out on the desk. It was difficult to identify location: with no urban context, the pictures protected James's geographical anonymity. But reviewed in chronological order, they disclosed the time line of his deceit . . .

The first picture was of James leaning against a white fence in the countryside. Horses were grazing in the background. The second photo was of the woman against the same fence. She was wearing a thick, tweedy outfit; and even at a distance, her gigantic brooch provided the details of silver thistles. Isabel concluded these two photographs of James and Suzie Evans were taken each by the other; and that James had reconnoitered with her in Ireland, after his visit to Annabel in London, where he must have placed his shoe order with Lobb.

The third photo was a blurred image of the underneath of James's chin. On its own, the botched photo seemed without importance. Juxtaposed against the subsequent photograph — of them together — it made sense. The woman's height was drolly out of scale with that of James: the top of her head barely reached the lower realms of his chest. Her height was now a reference point for the previous photo of James's chin wherein she had obviously been the photographer . . . that would explain the angle of the shot.

Isabel examined the last photo of them together. They were gazing down. What are they looking at? wondered Isabel. The object of their attention seemed to be the woman's left hand. Though it was not visible in the photo, Isabel realized they were looking at what must have been an engagement ring.

The fourth and fifth photos were of James and the woman together in what was presumably the Central Park rowboat.

Isabel looked at the dates again. The span from the photo of them gazing at her engagement ring until the one of them in the rowboat was five weeks. James had been engaged for five weeks before leaving the photos for Isabel to find. With any other man, Isabel wouldn't have believed that an engagement could occur within such an implausibly short period of time. But James had a pattern of proposing to women days after meeting them. He'd done exactly that with Isabel and her predecessor . . . why not again?

Isabel left the photographs on the desk and went into the bedroom. Laying supine on her made bed, Isabel closed her eyes and tried to remember whether she'd seen Suzie Evans before. The woman's inconsequential bearing revealed as little as her generic name. Isabel imagined James at the time the photos were taken. He had already remade himself by then. Five weeks ago James had given himself a fresh start with a tabula rasa provided by Suzie Evans . . . disappearing into a completely new world of people who didn't know Isabel. Perhaps those same people didn't know he was married, thought Isabel. If they did, they must be aware of James's intentions. How many people had known of James's intentions in the five weeks Isabel hadn't? Certainly the person who took the photograph of James and Suzie in Ireland, and of them in the Central Park rowboat. How many more knew? James's mother must have been among them. She knew at the time Isabel spoke to her. Like blood lapping onto the shores after the Peloponnesian Wars, one devastating realization led Isabel to another . . . and another, and another. While Isabel lay motionless on the bed, her entire being was replaced with sorrow so desolate, it denied tears.

Isabel got up from bed after a period of time she could not measure. She walked back to the desk, where the photographs were lined up in a single row, charting the sequential demise of her marriage. Pushing them aside, Isabel brought out a sheet of stationery.

Dear James,

I didn't understand your method of handling me until an ironic series of events today. Someone mistakenly thought I was the woman with you registered at a San Francisco hotel. I assume she's the same woman in the enclosed photographs.

One doesn't know what one knows any sooner than that moment. I know I tried and failed to change our marriage and its end, and what is left feels to me like a terrible hole. I know that you had a chance at truth, and you've chosen dishonesty.

I know without question that I loved you and therefore trusted you, and if you meant to hurt, you've done that more completely than could have been imagined.

We were lovers. We were married. We both cherish Burgo. We had a life together. We share friends. I'm re-solved to find integrity in our future relationship. I hope you can call on your own reasons to do the same.

Isabel removed her engagement ring and wedding band.

She wrapped them in tissue, and placed them inside a manila envelope, along with the letter and photographs.

Isabel sealed the envelope.

Spiraling grief engulfed her . . . and

Isabel began to drown.

49

Suzie Evans was neither attractive nor ugly nor anything else but rich.

She was the only child of a man who made a fortune in the poultry business in Petaluma, California. The Money was eventually moved into the trucking business, and then into shopping malls. Each time The Money was phased into an upgraded sector, it was made slightly more respectable. By the time Suzie was a debutante in San Francisco, her father had systematically reengineered The Money's provenance.

Like many women who have always been rich girls, Suzie was spoiled and insecure at the same time. Whatever happiness Suzie couldn't otherwise obtain, she bought — including husbands. Husband #1 was a penniless German duke who zeroed in on her like a heat-seeking missile. Daddy gave him go-away money two years into the marriage. Husband #2 was what James had dubbed the "shadow man," barely accounted for during the Versailles event fifteen years before. Too stupid or drunk to know not to walk behind a horse, he had been kicked in the head by a skittish polo pony. Three weeks into his coma, Shadow Man's respirator was turned off.

The day after he received Isabel's letter, James saw Suzie at the races in Paris. Her wealth had increased exponentially since they'd been introduced at the Versailles opera. Both of Suzie's parents had since died — most recently, her father. Suzie had inherited his fortune.

Suzie was in France to scatter her father's remains. But not all of them. His last wish was that his final resting place be on the Barbados estate, but Suzie had the idea of dispersing him in his favorite cities all over the world. It would involve destination travel, require different outfits, and, most important, it would give Suzie something to do.

Suzie's hair colorist once told her that Linda Porter always gave Cole a themed, jewel-encrusted cigarette case to mark each of his Broadway openings. Suzie decided she would do that too . . . or something like that. She would design a brooch to mark each time she cast her father's remains.

The first time was Barbados. It wasn't entirely successful. Suzie assumed that Daddy would come out of the urn in ashes. After all, that's what it was called . . . "ashes." She tipped the urn over her father's yacht, anchored in calm waters for the grave occasion, and he tumbled out as a combination of soot and cumbersome chunks. Not only did it look like the sweepings of a dirty chimney, too much of Daddy poured out all at once. At that rate, Suzie wouldn't have enough of him to go around. She thought of using a receptacle shaped like a large martini shaker so the pumicelike pieces of Daddy would be trapped before they rolled out. Then Suzie had a better idea. She instructed that whatever was left of her father be pulverized into a finer consistency. Asprey made an urn with a long neck deliberately pursed into a narrow opening. The second time — in Monte Carlo — was perfect. Daddy poured out in a thin gray line, which poetically dispersed just at the moment the breeze lifted him away.

Having finished scattering his dwindling remains in Biarritz, Suzie was in Paris to pick up her Gallic-themed brooch at Boucheron. She was reintroduced to James when they both happened to be at the Hippodrome for the races. As soon as James realized Suzie was available, his charm took over. He hovered attentively and listened with great interest. It proved to be no small effort, but James stayed on game.

Courtliness came naturally to James. He believed he was born a gentleman.

Life had granted James his station, and then, without reason, deprived him of real opportunity to utilize that advantage. Now, in the most unlikely of locations — at the Hippodrome in Paris — life seemed to be offering James a make-good.

Milling among those behind an area cordoned off from what would have been James without Suzie, James considered his odds. During their lunch at the Turf Club, a coolness of judgment set in. As the horses were turning into the final furlough of the fifth race, detachment had already overtaken James. By the time James escorted Suzie to dinner, he had made up his mind. It was raw self-interest. James decided to exchange his current situation for one with more advantages. James decided he would marry a woman he didn't love, because it would make his life better than staying married to the woman he did.

What was Suzie Evans thinking the day James was deciding to marry her? She was thinking Daddy was almost done. Afterward, she wasn't going anywhere. Ashford Castle in Ireland would be her last stop. Suzie was thinking, I need something next. Maybe James could be what she did next. Suzie heard he'd married the unaccessorized woman at the gala. If the woman's hairdo was any indication, no wonder the marriage isn't working out, she thought.

Suzie observed James as best she could from her low vantage point. He was interested in clothes, she could tell that. Suzie wasn't an intellect, but neither was she stupid; and there was something else Suzie could tell when she looked at James. She could tell James liked money.

James bought the engagement ring at a jewelry store on the avenue Mozart, within callous proximity to the café where he and Isabel had spent some part of every afternoon. Burgo was left with friends in Neuilly while his father flew to Ireland to propose to Suzie. It had been a remarkably short time — only three days — since James had seen her at the races. The rush by which James accomplished his marital transfer might have appeared vulgar to others — more a transaction than a courtship. In the larger scheme of things, propriety wasn't important. Not to James, at any rate. What was important to James was that he would be settled for life.

It wouldn't be a free ride. James understood he'd have his work cut out for him. But there would be diversions . . . there would be places to go and a private plane to take him there. There would be excellent wine to drink without a need to justify his enjoyment of it. There would be money to spend on beautiful things for which he need not make excuses.

James locked out any feelings for Isabel. It was the only way he could embark on his course. But nothing could be done to change the fact the same woman he evicted from himself would forever be the mother of his son. That inconvenient truth could not be disappeared.

50

It had been two days since Isabel sealed her own engagement ring in the envelope, along with the photographs and her letter. Two days since she last ate. Two nights since she last slept.

All of Isabel ached, each physical part insisting on its own hurt. Any sound, no matter how innocuous, was harsh to her ears. Her scalp stung when she combed her hair. When she brushed her teeth, her gums bled. Isabel's mental capacities were emptied out and replaced with excruciating lament. She couldn't think straight. Only when she realized Burgo was alone with her mother-in-law did Isabel call herself to action.

Not wishing to stay a single night under the same roof as Mrs. Willoughby, Isabel left the day she came to collect Burgo.

"Would you make sure your son receives this," said Isabel as she handed over the envelope. "Good-bye, Mrs. Willoughby."

"Papi is doing some unexpected travel," was how Isabel put it to Burgo. "I think Colonel should stay with Grammy until the end of the summer . . . that way, you and I can do some travel of our own without worrying about him."

Burgo made no objection. He made no remark. He was strangely reserved about the fact his father had disappeared, and his mother had just announced her intentions for travel to a yet-to-be-determined destination when he had only recently re-turned from living a year in a foreign country.

Isabel and Burgo finished unpacking whatever had been shipped from Paris to their new apartment in New York. As she obsessively arranged, and then rearranged, the apartment's rooms, Isabel felt more and more disenfranchised. The shape of James missing was in every room. James's absence had its own physical outline in bed and at the dinner table. Irrational as it was — despite his betrayal and her humiliation at not understanding the mechanics of it — Isabel longed for James. Anything in her view brought him back. Everything she thought included his wound-ing presence.

When Isabel was crazy with loss, he phoned.

In the fleeting moment between his announcement, "This is James," and what was to follow, Isabel held out hope. If she could, she would acquit him . . . he need only provide an opening.

"I'd like to see Burgo and collect some personal items," James announced stiffly.

"Can we talk?" asked Isabel.

"No. I'm uncomfortable with this."

"Are you saying you won't talk to me?"

"Not unless it has to do with Burgo."

"James . . ."

James repeated himself, as though reading from a script. "I'd like to see my son and collect my things."

Rather than let himself in with his key, James rang the downstairs buzzer and then knocked on the apartment's front door. He appeared faultlessly groomed in what looked to Isabel to be at least four thousand dollars' worth of bespoke English tailor-ing. James had traded up . . . right down to his eggplant-colored Italian socks. He was wearing a pair of Lobb shoes.

After a guarded conversation with Burgo, James found the cuff links his father had given to him. They were the only item he took from the apartment. The only words James had for Isabel concerned his clothes. He asked that all his clothes — every piece, including Isabel's gifts of sweaters and ties — be donated to All Saints Church, where Burgo had been christened.

Devastated by the lack of sentiment with which he cleaned out his closet, Isabel removed herself from sight until she heard James say good-bye to Burgo. Not wishing Burgo to see his father walk out alone, Isabel accompanied James downstairs to the street.

Even at that point, even when it was hopelessly over, Isabel would not passively allow love to slip away. She implored him to fight for the marriage, "Please let's at least shake hands."

"I'm sorry," is all he said, as he turned away and climbed into the back seat of the waiting limousine.

Burgo watched from the window two floors above as Isabel watched James — sealed in a tinted-windowed limousine — disappear in Fifth Avenue traffic.

As she walked back to the apartment, Isabel wondered how she would explain to her son what she couldn't possibly understand herself.

"Burgo, you and I should talk a bit. Come to the kitchen, and I'll make lemonade." Isabel deliberately chose a task — squeezing lemons — as a prop while they had their discussion.

"You know how your godmother Monina has a gift for insight?" asked Isabel.

"Yes . . . when I was little and we stayed with her, she told me stories. I've always thought of Monina as the good kind of witch," said Burgo.

Isabel pulled out the cutting board and began to halve the lemons. "She'd be flattered," she said. "Monina told me once that the worst pain comes when we try to hold on to something that was never there to begin with. I didn't want to hear, because she was talking about Papi. But she was right. I asked Papi to become responsible for himself, so he could become more responsible for us. I hoped he would change, but he didn't . . . not because he didn't want to, but because he couldn't. I was wrong all of these years to try to force Papi to become something he wasn't . . . to become something I wanted him to be."

Burgo listened with silent attention. Isabel wiped her hands and poured the bowl of juice into a pitcher of cold water. Burgo had his chance to say something. Instead, he took a tray of ice cubes out of the freezer.

"Thank you, sweetie, that's very helpful . . . now why don't you stir," Isabel said. She reached for the sugar, then handed Burgo a wooden spoon.

"It always takes forever for the sugar to melt," she said.

"If you had put sugar in with the lemon before adding the cold water, it would have made sugar syrup . . . and you wouldn't have the floating granules," Burgo pointed out.

"Burgo, I don't know what will become of Papi," said Isabel.

"I do," he stated calmly while he continued stirring.

"Do you?"

"I know he's left and won't be back."

"He won't come back here, but he'll come back for you," said Isabel. "And I'll have him back . . . not in the same way. In a way I'll keep quietly in my heart."

Burgo put down the wooden spoon. "Mommy, your heart is just a muscle. It's your mind that matters."

"I disagree. I think the head makes us reason, but the heart makes us human."

"Well, then it will only hurt you."

"Why would you say that?"

"Because I know where Papi has gone."

"You do?"

Burgo looked at his mother studiously. She seemed composed enough to hear what he had to say.

"Papi is flying off with someone."

"What an odd thing to say."

"It's true."

"How do you know?"

"Because when we were with Grammy after Paris, Papi gave me his cell phone and asked me to erase all of the messages."

Isabel's breath drew in sharply.

"I . . . I don't understand," she stuttered.

"You know how Papi can't handle any electronic equipment . . . he didn't know how to erase the phone messages, and so he asked me to. But in order to erase a message, you have to listen to it first. The messages were all from the same woman. They're getting married. She has her own plane. She must be very rich."

Whether by design or carelessness, James had asked Burgo to destroy evidence of infidelity. The Freudian breach of faith made forgiveness impossible. Whatever Isabel felt toward James had just been ruptured by her abhorrence.

So appalled was Isabel by what Burgo had just told her and that it was he who was telling her, she dared not trust what she'd say next.

"Mommy, are you all right?"

"It's just that I haven't had much sleep these last few days, and I think I need to lie down for a while," said Isabel.

Isabel shut the bedroom door and tried to take stock of whatever was left of her sanity. Since returning from Paris, she'd kept the entirety of her situation to herself. Not even the psychiatrist knew the whole story. She'd been careful to dole it out to him in partial chapters. Now the plot had suddenly turned frightening.

"Jesus, you should have killed the man in Paris when you had your chance," said Monina after Isabel phoned from behind the closed bedroom door.

"Why is he doing this?" cried Isabel in a muffled outburst. "How can he be doing this?"

"He believes he deserves it. That's why. And he's without shame. That's how. He's in survival mode. That's what makes him dangerous."

"What does he think when he looks in the mirror?" asked Isabel.

"He doesn't think anything," answered Monina. "You're confusing scruples with manners."

It was an unsparing assessment, which Isabel chose to ignore.

"There must be something," she insisted. "Something I haven't thought of yet . . . something I haven't seen."

"You're overanalyzing it," said Monina. "There's far less than meets the eye. Have you told your brother or father?"

"No. I haven't told anyone but you and a psychiatrist."

"You must have been in *really* bad shape to have turned to a psychiatrist, knowing what you think of them."

"I went to one because I couldn't remember why."

"Why what?"

"Why I tried to kill James."

"This just gets better and better. You couldn't remember the reasons you tried killing your husband?"

"Monina, sometimes I think I'm losing my mind."

"Christ, Isabel, the sadistic irony of your situation would have driven anyone else over the edge. You should be grateful there's a history of mental illness in your family . . . it's inoculated you against a more serious kind of insanity. I especially like the gods recasting Cassandra as a fact-checker."

Isabel didn't say anything.

"Isabel, are you still on the line?"

"Yes, I'm still here," said Isabel. "Monina, he knows what he's done. I'm sure of it."

"Of course he knows what he's done," said Monina. "He doesn't have a problem with it. You do. He doesn't."

"Why not?" asked Isabel. "Why not!"

"Well, I could tell you narcissism and self-deceit are indispensable to a drinker," said Monina. "Or I could just say what I think . . . that James is a luxury hound who's followed the money." Realizing it was a brutal shove, she softened the ground. "Isabel, my dear friend, literature is littered with characters like James. I know you can't possibly believe this now, but you're well out of it."

"What do mean by 'it'? 'It' was my life," Isabel said angrily.

"You'll have to sort that through on your own," said Monina.

Burgo knocked on the door.

"Mommy, are you awake? I heard you talking on the phone and thought you'd like a glass of lemonade."

51

W hy have you come back?" asked Dr. Lewis. "You told me our sessions were finished."

"I can't protect my son," said Isabel.

"From whom?"

"His father."

"Why would you need to?"

Isabel described Burgo's cell phone discovery. "What kind of man is James to have done that?" she asked.

"You tell me," suggested the doctor.

"I hate that Burgo feels the need to protect me."

"Let him . . . within reason. You both need to look after each other right now."

"How could it be possible that James left without facing me?"

"He thought it too unpleasant."

"I need more than glibness from you."

"I wasn't being glib."

"It was the worst kind of cowardice," said Isabel.

"But you still love him."

"I know it makes no sense . . ."

"You've somehow managed to separate esteem from love. Perhaps we should look into that."

Isabel's outward defiance took the place of what had been self-reflection. "I've had all the looking-into I can take," she shot back.

"All right . . ."

"Do you know anything about black holes, Doctor?"

"No more than a layman; only that they swallow matter."

"More than just matter . . . energy, light . . . the only thing they don't obliterate is information."

"I didn't know that. What's your point?"

"The basic tenet of modern physics is that it's always possible to reconstruct what happened . . . to retrieve information on how the dead star collapsed into a black hole. Or, in my case, how James could leave the way he did."

Dr. Lewis waited for something more.

"Come on, Doctor, with all of those advanced degrees, you should be getting this . . . the analogy is a fairly obvious one."

"I'm afraid I don't . . ."

"You do, but you want me to express it myself."

"You give me far too much credit. I really don't understand . . ."

"It's the gravitational pull of what James did," said Isabel. "It decimated truth and whatever orbits truth: decency, honor, reciprocity . . . all sucked into the black hole."

"So?" asked Dr. Lewis.

"So I refuse to look into the abyss. In fact, I'm doing the opposite of 'looking into.' I'm leaving. I'm leaving the country . . . for a while, at any rate."

"Where will you go?"

"I've no idea," Isabel said as she stood up.

"There's another fifteen minutes to the session."

"I think we're finished."

"All right then, good luck to you, Isabel," said the doctor as he shook her hand.

"It's overdue," said Isabel.

A great imperial capital for sixteen centuries — first of the Byzantine Empire and then of the Ottoman sultans — Istanbul straddles Europe and Asia. It's divided not only by the Bosporus, but also by vast epochs of history. They stayed in the Pera Pala Hotel for two reasons, both literary. Burgo loved Agatha Christie, who'd written *Murder on the Orient Express* in Room 411; and Isabel was feeling especially drawn to the itinerant Lord Byron, who once lived in Pera.

In the mornings, Isabel and Burgo took a shaky wood-and-wrought-iron lift down to the faded elegance of the hotel's breakfast room. A jarring combination of strong tea and patisserie charged them with enough artificial energy for hours of exploring the city. The first and second days were spent among the masques and palaces; the third, in the mazes of winding, covered streets crammed with hundreds of tiny shops within the Grand Bazaar and the Spice Market.

After washing away the dust of their morning, Isabel and Burgo would have another tea, this time in the hotel's salon. Surrounded by sweet cakes, they sat in comfortable period chairs and read: Burgo with his nose in an Agatha Christie mystery, Isabel sampling Lady Wortley Montagu's 1817 diary, which described the Ottoman society during her husband's tenure as British ambassador.

"What will I do when I've run out of Agatha Christie?" asked Burgo with his mouth full of halvah.

"You'll still have plenty of reading left."

"But she's my favorite."

"I promise there'll be other favorites."

"Do you like your book, Mommy?"

"It's very interesting."

"That's what you say when you learn something but don't enjoy the book."

"You're right."

"So what have you learned?"

"Well, I've learned that the sultan's mother presided over his harem."

Isabel looked at her son, who put down his halvah to give the subject his total attention.

"I won't be managing yours, Burgo. You should understand that right now."

The last day in Istanbul, Isabel took pains to find the Mevlevi Monastery, tucked away behind crumbling ancient buildings in an eighteenth-century lodge, within which, on a beautiful octagonal wooden dance floor, the Sufis whirl themselves into a state of ecstatic communication with Allah. As she watched the dervishes spin around and around and into a trance, Isabel found her own act of will. *I won't be thinking of James by tomorrow,* she repeated over and over again. *By tomorrow's call to prayer, James will not be in me.*

But the next morning, when Isabel and Burgo packed to return to New York, James hadn't weakened his hold on Isabel's thoughts . . . and he still held sway over her heart. As all of Istanbul faced Mecca to pray, James remained stubbornly a part of Isabel.

52

When will it be over?" Isabel asked her brother when she phoned several weeks after returning from Istanbul.

"I still can't bring myself to walk near the rowing pond in Central Park. I sleep across the bed so there's no empty space on the side James is meant to be. I've been afraid Burgo will hear when I cry, so I hold it in until I can drown out the noise with my baths. After months of crying only when I turn on water — like the default panel in a Skinnerian experiment — I thought I had myself under control. And then, one afternoon, I lost it when I heard a Chet Baker song on the radio. Burgo had one uninterrupted hour of watching his mother fall apart. God only knows how far that must have set him back. I hate it. When will it end?"

"It takes a cow three days," said Ian.

"Isabel . . . are you there?" Ian asked when he didn't hear any response.

"What in God's name did you just say?" Isabel demanded.

"Cows," said her brother.

"What the hell do cows have to do with my situation?"

"When a calf dies on her watch, a cow stands in the exact spot for three days," explained Ian. "She doesn't move. She doesn't eat. She just stands there, in the same spot she last saw her calf alive. Then . . . it's the most remarkable thing, Izzie, on the third day, she just walks away."

"So?"

"It's nature's way of allowing a grieving period, but putting an end to it so the cow comes into heat and reproduces again. I'm sure there's some kind of nonbovine version of that . . . they say it takes people twenty-one days to break a habit and a year to recover from tragedy."

"What possible difference will a year make?" asked Isabel.

"Everything changes in time and looks different from a distance," said Ian.

"That's not true . . . that's just not true. The distance between me and James can be measured in thousands of miles, but it's been impossible to disentangle myself from him. I keep waiting for him to be gone — for time to take him away. Each week there's some different rendition of the same awfulness."

"What was it this week?' asked Ian.

"Friends who phone with the 'I just can't believe it' conversation . . . as though they expect *me* to explain it to *them*. God, I can't face any more outrage on my behalf."

"It could be worse," suggested Ian.

"How? How can it possibly be worse?"

Ian tried to think of an example that included human participants this time.

"Well, I read something once in a medical journal. It was this case in Canada . . . a freak accident between two men in a fencing tournament. The tip of one man's foil managed to go through the other's face mask. It's difficult to believe, but it went up his nostril and pierced his brain, damaging some uncharted area that destroyed the man's ability to remember emotional pain. Each time he heard something sad — about his wife's death, for example —

he would react with the same intense feeling he had the first time he heard it. It was as though the first time was the first time forever."

"Tell me you're kidding, Ian."

"What?"

"Your anthropomorphic cow story, and then a case review from the *New England Journal of Medicine*. Can't you come up with reassurance that doesn't involve the stockyard or Austrian fencing accidents?"

"Canadian . . . the accident was in Canada. And I'm just saying it could be worse," Ian said in his defense. "Do you want me to stay with you for a while?"

"Thanks for the offer, but I can't picture you in New York. In another few days, I'll be in a new job, and Burgo starts school."

"How is he?"

"Quiet."

"I wouldn't worry too much . . . he's never been a talker."

"Burgo is a blessed distraction," admitted Isabel. "When I'm not feeling guilty about that, I'm feeling overwhelmed by what he'll need from me."

"He'll take what he needs from you, and find the rest somewhere else. Children are far more resilient than adults," suggested Ian.

"I know, but I still worry," said Isabel. "I looked into his room the other night. There was this jumble of long legs and arms with enormous feet hanging off the bed. He's not a boy anymore, and I have these waves of panic. God, I hope I do the right thing by him. It's so easy to foul up."

"You'll know when to bring Burgo closer to you, and when to let go," Ian reassured his sister. "Mothers can raise sons without fathers."

"I hope I'm not bringing my own unhappiness into his life," said Isabel.

"Well, it's a desperately unhappy situation, and you can't protect him from that. But it won't stay unhappy. You'll see. Have you spoken to Father yet?"

"I don't want a lecture."

"Give him a chance. You might be surprised."

At the same time Isabel was contemplating the relationships between mothers and sons, arrangements were being made for Mrs. Willoughby to receive a first-stage funding from hers. It had been agreed that, as soon as James and Suzie married, the Willoughby place would be completely renovated.

Suzie owned a gleaming white Maurice Fatio-designed mansion situated between the Bath and Tennis Club and Sloan's Circle in Palm Beach. James was surrounded by everything material; but nothing was entirely his. His would be the Willoughby estate. The Money would return James's ancestral home to its original splendor. James thought the Pugin sideboard, one of several wedding gifts from Suzie, would show magnificently in the refurbished dining room.

Suzie and James's lives would triangulate among their various residences, each seasonally scheduled for agreeable weather and social activities. Spring and fall would be spent on the Willoughby estate; winter, in Palm Beach and Barbados; they would summer in Saratoga. Colonel never made it to New York. He was kept in Virginia; his Hermès collar had been replaced with one embedded with a computer chip, which sounded an alert each time he strayed. James was also fitted with a control device . . . an ironclad prenuptial agreement.

The wedding invitations were being printed by Smythson. Suzie had already placed an order with Leontine Linens for a monogram change on her pillowcases and towels. The only loose end was Isabel. James left that detail to Suzie as well.

Suzie remembered Isabel from the Versailles gala years ago. What Isabel lacked in jewelry and the right hairdresser, she more than made up in confidence, thought Suzie. She decided she'd better not leave anything to chance: Suzie chose the most aggressive in her flotilla of lawyers to deal with the possibility of a vindictive ex-wife.

The separation agreement included the misspelling of Isabel's last name. It arrived at the on-sale date of the magazine wherein James's article heralded his blissfully long-lasting marriage to Isabel. That wasn't the last of the ironies.

"Has James seen this document?" Isabel asked Robert Gallagher after she read it in his office.

"According to his attorney's cover letter, he has."

Isabel was incredulous.

"He's supplied an inventory of personal property, right down to the salad forks," said Robert.

"James's memory is too faulty for inventory lists," insisted Isabel.

"Apparently not when it comes to his possessions. . . . Isabel, you'd better face the unseemly facts. He's making the distinction between marital property and his own," said Robert. "And there's more."

"How could there possibly be more? It's grotesquely thorough," said Isabel.

"They've included a noninterference clause."

"What in God's name is that?"

"It prevents you from stalking either of them."

Legalities put Isabel in her place, and on her own with Burgo. The divorce would be final in a year.

Monina had to joke, "Your virtue had better be its own reward, because nothing else is."

Hours after Isabel signed the separation document, she received an e-mail from James:

> With your cooperation, I wish to complete our unpleasant task and accomplish a Haitian divorce.

Isabel yanked the self-preservation ripcord. She phoned her father.

There was jaw-twitching silence on the other line after Isabel described the points included in the separation agreement and James's request for a twenty-four-hour divorce.

"It's the Dominican Republic, for Christ's sake," Rufus said. He was seething. "Haiti doesn't have a government these days, let alone a legal process. I guess that's the kind of news not covered by the *Racing Form*."

"Daddy, *please,* try to be more helpful. What do I do?"

"Don't give it to him. Arrogant bastard. Jesus wept . . . you've yet to be introduced to the woman, and she'd become Burgo's stepmother in the same twenty-four hours. Do you even know her name?"

"Suzie Evans."

"Of Evans Poultry?"

"I have no idea . . . yes, I think so . . . chickens."

"It must be the same Evans. Her father was a ruthless son of a bitch."

"So are you, Daddy. I'm hoping that might work to my advantage. God knows, nothing else has."

Rufus laughed dryly. "I'm glad you haven't lost your sense of humor."

"It's my courage I'm afraid of losing. I have this dreadful feeling that with that kind of money, there aren't any boundaries . . . that anything can happen."

"Nothing will happen unless you want it to. Don't cooperate with him. Don't communicate with him. And don't let it eat away at you," Rufus instructed his daughter.

Isabel thought her father was done talking, but he started to say something else.

"Isabel. I wasn't —" He stopped himself.

"You weren't what?" asked Isabel.

"It's not important," said her father.

In fact, it was.

4

With the help of Augustinian nuns,
Isabel remembered the rest . . .

53

James's brief phone message to Burgo took up the entire spool of tape on Isabel's answering machine.

It was the first time in months Isabel had heard James's voice. Her eyes began to well. She reached down to hit the skip button on the answering machine; but before her finger landed, Isabel realized James hadn't hung up the phone on his end. What had been recorded, unbeknownst to him, was the continuation of his life after what he thought was a short hello to Burgo. Isabel's prelude to tears was instantly replaced with an audio version of voyeurism.

There was another man's voice solicitously asking whether the call had gone through. Then there was a distant sound of . . . what? A liquid thud. Then sounds of splashing water . . . splashing that progressively became louder.

Isabel's brain moved forward in a series of clipped deductions.

The splashes were deep and rhythmic. Someone in a swimming pool. James in a swimming pool. There was no other splashing. No one else in the pool. Just James.

It must be a private pool. A pool at one of Suzie's houses. A house in a warm climate. Barbados. James had made the call from poolside. The butler dialed for him and then handed him the phone. After James left his message for Burgo, the butler reappeared to ask if the call went through. He assumed James had turned off the phone.

Isabel smiled to herself. He still doesn't know how to handle the phone, she thought. The phone, which had not been shut off and was left on the table, acted as a recording device. As Isabel listened, it occurred to her that for the first time since he'd left her standing on the curb, they were together. The call had been placed sometime that morning, so it wasn't in real time; and James had no idea he was being recorded. Still, Isabel felt a strange type of connection with him by way of sound effects.

Isabel assumed the rest of the tape would consist of more lap sounds. He's out of shape, she thought when she heard James coming out of the pool after only swimming the lap toward the phone. She waited for more. There were muffled towel sounds. And then James called out a name.

When James called out to Suzie, it yanked Isabel back into the present tense.

Isabel's tears queued once again, but something stopped her a second time from crying. It was the sound of prattling words from Suzie, along with hollow ones belonging to James. The banality of their conversation sapped Isabel's resolve to listen to any more.

Before hearing the tape, Isabel had convinced herself there was more to James and his story. Monina might have been right. Maybe there was less. What words had James used in his e-mail? He wished to conclude their "unpleasant task" of divorcing. What kind of word was *unpleasant*? And how could anyone with the slightest depth refer to a divorce as a *task*? Isabel thought back to the other casual words belonging to James. She remembered he once thanked her for being "gracious" when she had no choice but to pay the outstanding bills . . . as though balancing the checkbook was a social event. Two words that had held prominent places in his vocabulary were "amused" and "annoyed." Both described surface.

Perhaps that was all James had ever wanted for himself. Marriage to Isabel had stretched the surface of James. Something — some slight last pull — had torn it. Perhaps James was where he had always wanted to be: in a warm climate having an undemanding conversation with a woman who had a low threshold of expectation.

Isabel reached over to the machine. She pressed the erase button.

54

It had been six months.

In the mornings, Isabel still woke with a leaden feeling. Afraid to be left alone with her thoughts during the day, she immersed herself in work. In the middle of the night, the worst of Isabel's unaccountable fears forced her bolt upright with an overwhelming anxiety that whatever she provided her son came only to one-half of his parental needs.

Eventually, the bite of Isabel's fear receded. Eventually, Isabel and Burgo found ways to manage their own lives and their lives together. More and more, there were boisterous discussions between the two of them and among friends. On rare occasions, the gods gave Isabel unconscious moments of joy.

There had been no mail from James until the package.

Burgo came into the kitchen with it splayed open. Isabel was preparing dinner.

"What's in the package, sweetie?" asked Isabel.

"Ties."

"How nice. Was there a note?"

"No. Just ties. A great many, actually."

"How many?"

"Seven."

Isabel, just about to cook pasta, turned off the stove.

"Seven? Why so many?"

"It stands to reason," said Burgo, who proceeded to lay the facts out on the kitchen counter.

Burgo had scrutinized the reverse sides of the ties. "The store for all but one is English," he said. "They probably had lunch in London on Monday because the package was sent from Burlington Arcade overnight, and the Federal Express receipt is dated two days ago."

Isabel sat on the kitchen stool.

"I have no proof, but I'm sure they had lunch and then couldn't think of anything to do," said Burgo. "So what do you do after lunch when you have nothing else to do?" he asked.

"I can't honestly remember when I last had time for a long lunch," said Isabel. "I certainly don't remember when I had nothing to do. I should very much like to experience both, though."

"You shop," explained Burgo. "And how many ties do you buy when you have more than enough money?"

"As many as there are different colors?"

"That's right. What's more, they must have traveled to London from Palm Beach," he added.

Isabel got up and turned on the stove. "I'm almost afraid to ask . . ."

"It's elementary," said Burgo. "One of the ties isn't new. It has a Palm Beach label. Papi saw a tie he liked for himself while he was shopping for mine in London. He took off the tie he bought in Palm Beach. Either he didn't want to carry the new one, or he'd tired of the old one. He put on the new tie and included the old tie in my package."

"Very impressive deduction, Sherlock. And now *it stands to reason* you wash your hands and set the table, because dinner will be ready in another twenty minutes," said Isabel, who, truth be told, was remembering a similar story with a different main character, one which had been Burgo's favorite as a baby. Babar . . . his trip to the tailor, courtesy of the rich woman.

Several weeks after he sent the ties, James phoned Burgo with plans to introduce him to his future stepmother.

"You know you don't have to do anything that makes you uncomfortable," said Isabel.

"I know," replied Burgo. "But I need to see this for myself so I don't keep wondering about it."

The buzzer sounded the day he was being picked up. Burgo kissed his mother good-bye.

"Do you have plans?" he asked.

"I'm visiting Tessa in the country. I'll be back Sunday afternoon. I've written the phone number on a piece of paper and put it in your toilet kit. Call if you need to talk."

"I'll be fine," Burgo reassured his mother.

"I'm sure you will," she said.

There were no questions . . . nothing discussed between Isabel and Burgo when they both returned on Sunday afternoon. Burgo's sole comment was a thick black line, straight and to the point.

"It looks like what it is," he said.

With the evidence of sophisticated brain scan images, researchers have argued that the emotion of love is closer in its neural profile to hunger, thirst, or drug cravings . . . and that the intellectual construct of love operates on the same axis as homeostatic rewards such as food and warmth. When the object of love is removed

abruptly while one is still in love, what flares up first is so emotionally violent, it feels almost like a physical withdrawal. Then
the brain settles into a less extreme — but nonetheless active —
mode, quelled only by the passage of time.

Isabel was coming off withdrawal from James, but her long-
ing for him continued to make itself known with feelings of
melancholy and restlessness. Whenever Burgo's school schedule
and her own allowed, they left the country for foreign adventure,
often departing on the spur of the moment for long weekends in
whatever European cities offered out-of-season prices.

While she wandered among the Goya paintings in the Prado,
Burgo happily occupied himself in the museum's garden. He spotted a black cat in the bushes and decided that if — in each foreign
city they visited — he saw another black cat, he would return to
that exact same spot as an adult. In one year's time, Burgo had followed a black cat around on San Giorgio Maggiore while Isabel
admired the Tintorettos. He found one sleeping on a pile of books
at Shakespeare & Company in the Latin Quarter. And he shared an
overstuffed couch with one at Brown's Hotel in London. Burgo
enjoyed the admiration of black cats abroad; and Isabel was, with
each new city, feeling less of the sharp tip to her sadness.

Graham Greene, that peripatetic womanizer, suggested another way a man took trips was to have affairs. With each new
woman there were different customs, a foreign landscape, and a
changed way of life. During Isabel's post-James journeys, she often
met women who had been James's pre-Isabel travel. In London,
one volunteered she'd been engaged to James before her father in-
tervened. Another, in New York, admitted she'd been engaged to
James as well. James had changed his mind and decamped to
Virginia, where he didn't return her calls or acknowledge her let-

ters. The woman said the oddest thing was that when James finally returned to New York, he acted as if nothing had happened, including the marriage proposal.

In Santa Barbara, a woman who sat across from Isabel at a dinner party announced she had been with James some twenty years ago. Their relationship came to an abrupt end when, one afternoon, she appeared unannounced.

"I knew he'd just slept with another woman," she said.

Even for southern California, it was an overly personal disclosure. All heads at the table swirled in her direction.

"Do you know how I knew?" the woman asked Isabel and, now it seemed, the other guests.

Before Isabel could say that she had the need not to know, the woman answered her own question. "There was a condom stuck to the wall."

Everyone stopped eating. The woman misunderstood their silence for confusion and took a further step to clarify.

"He must have flung it against the wall . . . you know, in his rush to get rid of the evidence . . . and it stuck. I came into the room . . . there was this thing on the wall opposite the bed."

Embarrassment washed over the table. Still, the woman persisted. "Can you imagine?" she asked.

No one person there could have previously imagined; but now, all of them could.

The more Isabel learned of James's history with women, the more she wondered about something her father had once started to say but hadn't. The next time they spoke, she made a point of asking.

"Daddy, when I phoned you after James asked for a twenty-four-hour divorce, you wanted to tell me something but stopped yourself. Do you remember?"

"Yes," said Rufus.

"I need to know what that was."

"Why is it important now?"

"It just is."

"All right. I started to tell you that shortly before you and James were married, he suggested a wedding gift of one of my paintings."

"Are you serious?"

"He didn't ask for it outright; but he certainly made it known he wanted the picture. That was the point I decided —"

"Just tell me you didn't have James tailed by a detective," interrupted Isabel.

"Of course I didn't have him tailed. What would be the point of that? I ran a background check. I'd have warned you if he had had a criminal record."

"Well, I suppose that's something," said Isabel.

"I had someone ask around," said Mr. Simpson. "James was borderline disreputable . . . but I decided not to tell you."

"Why not?" asked Isabel

Isabel had always thought of her father as cynical. He proved her wrong.

"Because you were in love with him," said Rufus Simpson. "And people sometimes change."

55

Suzie staged her wedding to James in Saratoga.

"It's happening the weekend of the horse sales," announced Rebecca, who received an invitation. "I ask you, could there possibly be more appropriate a setting?"

"I'd prefer not hearing about it," insisted Isabel.

"We've all made a bad choice at some point," offered Rebecca sympathetically.

"James wasn't a bad choice . . . not when I made it."

"You can't mean that."

"Actually, I do."

"But look what he did! And how he did it!"

"He made a mess of it," admitted Isabel. "But what explains me? Where was I in all of this?"

"You were doing your best."

"Maybe he was too," said Isabel. "Maybe he couldn't do any more than he did. Rebecca, remember years back . . . the first time you and I talked about James writing a novel? Even then, we agreed he was his best writing short. I was the long story. I was what he couldn't do, and he knew it."

"He should have tried harder," said Rebecca. "You were a family. Everything begins and ends there."

"There was a failure on my part," said Isabel.

"How can you sit there and say that?" asked Rebecca.

"Come on . . . I can't claim money was the unspoken marker. James said it over and over again. I refused to listen, and failed to see."

"Isabel. I wasn't going to tell you this . . . I ran into them a few days ago, coming out of Cipriani," said Rebecca.

"Don't . . . ," implored Isabel.

"I want to say something, and then I'll never bring him up again. I swear."

"Keep it short."

"Okay," said Rebecca. "How's this for short: She looks like work. From the little I saw of them, he'll be earning every nickel."

"That's enough, Rebecca."

Rebecca continued to flog her point. "Some part of him is missing, Isabel, some part of his soul. And what's left is for hire," she said.

"How can you be so sure yours is the better morality?" asked Isabel. "I forced James to make a decision. Can you honestly claim you wouldn't have made the same practical choice?"

"I'd like to think I wouldn't compromise myself," said Rebecca.

"How many women do we know who've married for money?" interrupted Isabel.

"It's not the same thing," said Isabel.

"Why not?"

"It just isn't."

"Of course it is."

"It's unmanly," insisted Rebecca.

"Unmanly in this country . . . but not necessarily among Europeans," suggested Isabel. "They seem to have a less sentimental take on the subject."

Rebecca's face lit up. "Isabel, you should write a modern-day Edith Wharton novel. God knows, you have the material."

"You're not serious."

"I certainly am. Why not?"

"Because I can't put it into words. And even if I could, it's more than I can tell. All I know is that the meaning of my marriage isn't inscribed in its last chapter."

Isabel and Burgo were out of the country for James's wedding. They went to Rome. Before they left, Isabel received a letter from Monina.

> Thin girl,
>
> Before leaving Rome, visit its oldest church in the early evening. The door to the convent is on the left in the third courtyard. Go inside and ring the bell on the opposite wall. Ask the nun for the key to the chapel. Be sure and walk through the last arch in the courtyard before six o'clock.
>
> A part of your life is over. Another has begun. Find your way from one to the other. It would be a mistake otherwise.

Burgo wanted to be as close to the Pantheon as possible. He was sure it would improve his odds of spotting a black cat. They stayed at the Hotel Nazionale on the Piazza Montecitorio, which had a long history with writers. Isabel requested Room 312, where Simone de Beauvoir and Jean-Paul Sartre had often stayed. Burgo was given a small room on the fourth floor.

"There's something I need to do without you," Isabel explained to Burgo on their second day. "I'll be back for dinner.

Here are ten euros if you get hungry. I don't want you wandering too far away from the piazza."

The basilica of Santi Quattro Coronati is dedicated to four crowned martyrs who were artists. It is the oldest church in Rome and hides behind the high stone walls of a fortified castellated building. The entrance gate of the monastery is beneath the campanile. At five-thirty, Isabel rang the bell. A trapdoor in the wall opened briefly, then was closed, then opened again. A large key was shoved through. Isabel unlocked the door to the right of the portico. The tiny chapel was so dark, she had to feel her way to the light switch. When she turned it on and looked up, Isabel saw the most remarkable Byzantine frescos covering the walls.

The first panel depicted Constantine suffering from leprosy. Two saints appear in his dream and urge the sick emperor to seek Pope Sylvester in Rome. He journeys there on the back of a donkey. The pope cures him by dunking him in a basin. A grateful Constantine gives the pope his crown. The pope rides off. On his own journey, the pope recovers a piece of the true cross. He brings a wild bull back to life. He liberates the Romans from a dragon. Isabel studied the dragon in the last panel. She thought of Ian.

Isabel walked through the last archway of the courtyard just as Augustinian nuns, most of them very old, and only a few very young, filed through. Theirs was a vow of silence, and so none of them objected when Isabel followed them into the church and sat down on an empty pew. A priest came in. Isabel noticed that the oldest nun, who resembled a character from a Daumier drawing, came to life when the man appeared. Her ancient curved back had long ago bowed her head, limiting her view to the ground below her feet. As the priest passed by her, she tilted her face up and smiled at what might have been the only man allowed within the convent.

Between men and women, it will always be, thought Isabel.

The nuns recited all twenty decades of the Rosary. They re-peated Santa Maria in a hypnotic drone that reminded Isabel of the Sufis' strange chants. There was a long pause. Isabel, assuming they were in silent prayer, stood to leave just as the nuns began to sing. It was completely unexpected and breathtakingly beautiful. Isabel couldn't understand the words. They were in Latin. That didn't matter.

56

Burgo was fifteen.

Three years had passed since he watched his father disappear. Once James had accessed The Money, he reappeared and invited Burgo to share in it. But Burgo stayed behind. He stayed behind and saved his mother simply by being her son.

Isabel knew that Burgo had shown her a way back to hope. In what would be her most difficult act of selflessness, she let him go.

"It's time you become the author of your own story," she told him.

Isabel and Burgo waited for James in front of the admissions office at Andover.

Isabel thought she'd finally have the chance to look into James's eyes, and he would be forced to take her into account. But nothing remained of the person Isabel knew to be James. She watched her son and his father go into the yellow clapboard building.

Burgo decided not to attend Andover, despite Willoughby tradition. He went to another school. When Isabel packed his school trunk, she remembered the earthquake kit she'd filled before he left for first grade . . . and that she had placed a photograph on top of the dehydrated food.

Isabel thought to include something of her own in Burgo's trunk. It was brought down — along with two other items — from the very back of the top shelf in her closet. Without unwrapping it, Isabel placed it in the trunk with a note.

> Dearest, dear boy,
>   When the others in your school ask how you came to possess such an extraordinary snakeskin, tell them your father brought it out of the Amazon jungle.

One of the other two keepsakes was a large envelope with three drawings: self-portraits by the three of them made when Burgo was little. Isabel's self-deprecating portrait was of her in a frantic state with her hair on fire. Burgo drew himself as the Monkey God, one of his favorite stories at that age. James's self-portrait was far more detailed. James drew himself drawing himself. In the mirrored moment he drew it, the artist was James dressed in a pajama top and briefs with pen in hand . . . standing in front of his counterpart, who was posed heroically, with a dog by his side, in front of a mansion. Isabel realized that the mansion was a renewed version of the Willoughby manor house; and that the dog was both Colonel and Admiral . . . the same dog in the auctioned-off painting. James had signed the drawing, "JW depicting self." Like the others, it'd been dated the day it was drawn.

For the last three years, Isabel had convinced herself that when James sold out, he lost his way. As she studied his self-portrait of some ten years ago, it occurred to her that maybe it was the opposite. Maybe, instead of losing his way, James had finally found it. How many times had she heard him say, "When I get rich," in the years they were together? Those words had been the impossible-seeming truth.

What if that's where James was going when he met her . . . before he fell in love with her? What if she wasn't James's destination but the unexpected stop along the way?

Isabel unwrapped the last item taken down from the closet shelf. It was the pair of silver spurs that had been Ian's wedding present. She brought them to the desk and rewrapped a single spur. It would go to James. In the letter she included — in her last letter to him — Isabel would do her best with words.

> The part of you that I still hold dear is the part with which
> I write
>> Dear James . . .

An editor will tell you that suspending disbelief is the mark of good fiction. James did that . . . up to the very moment he left Isabel.

Burgo had spotted it long ago. "Papi is fiction, and you are fact," he'd said once as a small boy.

It was Isabel, not James, who traveled the world. James, a travel writer when she first met him, was now moving in society's constricted radius. Suzie's prenuptial agreement kept James in velvet bondage, but he was becoming more and more detached. That unattractive fact didn't escape Suzie, who was beginning to tire of James's indifference toward her.

Isabel promised Burgo a trip to Bangkok during Christmas vacation of his first year in boarding school. They took an overnight flight. Burgo fell asleep as soon as the plane settled into its altitude. Isabel couldn't sleep. Pitch-dark suspended her in time and place, setting off echoes of the past. She remembered the last morning James and she had been together. Days, weeks, and months later, when Isabel had finally begun to understand and then was forced to fully comprehend James's deceptions, what haunted her the most — more than every other duplicity — what tortured her with gnawing self-doubt, was the ignorance of her impending doom while they made love.

Why would a man make love to a woman he knew he was leaving a few hours later? The Rebeccas of the world would say James did it because he could. They would say that Isabel should have known.

Isabel hadn't known. Not those things. She had known other things.

Before James lost his conscience, before Isabel lost her heart, before Burgo lost his patrimony, James had willingly given the full measure of love. It came at an unforgettable cost — scraping Isabel down to the marrow of her bones. Calling into question everything she believed important. Stealing hope and leaving her with annihilating grief.

Love at its worst had forced the worst of Isabel on herself; and then it denied her an explanation. When Isabel could finally remember, she became afraid of a more permanent loss . . . a loss without recovery: the loss of recalling James when she adored him beyond reason . . . when, at its best, love had been its own reward.

Isabel switched on the overhead light. The stewardess came down the aisle to offer a glass of water.

"Do you have the right time?" asked Isabel.

"For which day?" asked the stewardess, who explained they'd just crossed the dateline.